JASMINE FLORENTINE
ILLUSTRATED  EBONY GLENN

Library of Congress Control Number: 2022937987
ISBN 9781943147779; 9781943147786; 9781943147793

Written by Jasmine Florentine
Illustrated by Ebony Glenn
Project Journal written and illustrated by Jasmine Florentine
Text and Project Journal © 2022 Jasmine Florentine
Interior Art © 2022 The Innovation Press
Published by The Innovation Press
7511 Greenwood Avenue N. #4132, Seattle, WA 98103
www.theinnovationpress.com

Printed and bound by Worzalla
Production date June 2022

Cover art by Ebony Glenn
Book layout by Tim Martyn

In loving memory of my mom, Barbara Florentine, and my aunt, Teri Merliss, who filled my life with love, music, and a lot of laughter.

MIDBAR

THE GREAT BARREN

MT. DESIRE

PIXBIE

NO MAGIC GIRL

If Hex were a normal kid, she wouldn't be dragging the heavy kitchen stool into the yard, stumbling every time it got caught on a clod of dirt or in a glow-mole hole. If she were normal, she could wave a hand and say the right word and the stool would slide over the grass to where she needed it. But she wasn't normal, so she kept going, the coil of rope over her shoulder already slipping.

She glanced furtively down the road that passed in front of their yard and was relieved to see that it was empty. She didn't need one of her old classmates passing by to watch her struggle. They were probably all busy preparing for the first day of school tomorrow anyway.

Her six-year-old brother, Spanner, trailed behind her, cradling her sketchbook in one arm and her bag and an old scarf in the other. Their cat, Queen Fuzzybutt III, bounded after them, chasing the spot of light reflected from the metal clasp on Hex's sketchbook.

"You ready to build this thing?" Hex asked, dumping the rope and stool in the shade of their favorite tree.

"Yes!" Spanner jumped up and down. "Wait, no! You have to tell the story first!"

"Which story is that?" She already knew which one, of course. It was the inspiration for today's project.

He unclasped her sketchbook and rifled through the pages, his small face creased in concentration. The book was filled with hundreds of pictures Hex had drawn over the years to illustrate her stories. Spanner's face broke into a delighted smile as he held up the book. "The one about No Magic Girl and the ogre!"

"Oh, *that* story!" Hex said, pretending to be surprised. It was one of the first stories Hex had ever told Spanner, and she'd repeated it only about five thousand times since.

They flumped down onto the grass and Spanner laid the sketchbook open in front of them, handling it like a precious relic. Queen Fuzzybutt III leapt into Hex's lap and curled into a little ball. Her milk-white fur started glowing pink as she purred. Hex ran her fingers across the cat's back, now crimson, and warm as fresh-baked bread.

"Once upon a time," Hex began, "there was a girl who was different from all the other kids. They could make light with a single incantation or instantly freeze a glass of water. But this girl couldn't do any of those things. She couldn't make flowers change colors or levitate a frog above the ground. This girl was—"

"No Magic Girl," Spanner breathed. Hex stifled a giggle at Spanner's solemn reverence. Creative naming had not been one of eight-year-old Hex's talents, but it was four years too late to change it now.

"That's right," she continued. "Even though No Magic Girl couldn't do magic, she could do all sorts of other things, like make a fire with nothing but rock and steel, or turn a perilous fall into a gentle float to the ground using only a big piece of cloth. But her parents worried about her—without magic, they thought she wouldn't be able to survive in the world on her own. No Magic Girl knew better. You see, when her parents weren't watching, she went adventuring all by herself!

"One day, No Magic Girl ran away to the Cloud Mountains, where the ancient legends say there was hidden treasure. But barely a mile outside of town, what did she encounter?"

"A sleeping ogre!" Spanner squealed.

"Ten times bigger than an elephant but a hundred times meaner and uglier! As soon as he heard No Magic Girl's footsteps down the road, the ogre's eyes flew open, and he sat up. She tried to run, but it was too late. The ogre grabbed her and took her back to his cave. He put her on his table and locked the door. 'Don't even try to escape!' he boomed. 'There's a curse on my cave, so it's impossible to use magic. Tomorrow morning, I'm going to eat you for breakfast!'"

Spanner's eyes and mouth went round in suspense, then genuine fear. "Hex, what if an ogre comes here? Will you fight it?"

"They live in the mountains, Spanner. I think we'll be okay."

"But what if one of them gets hungry and comes down from the mountains?" he pressed.

"Then a brave warrior like the Thunder Knight will stop it," Hex replied. The Thunder Knight was Spanner's second favorite hero, after No Magic Girl. But unlike her, the Thunder Knight was actually a real person and more importantly, the most famous, brave, and powerful adventurer in the whole world.

Spanner still looked nervous, so Hex rolled her eyes with exaggeration. "Spanner, you need to get *ogre* it."

Spanner's jaw dropped, clearly affronted that his sister would dismiss his worries. Then the pun clicked and he burst out laughing, his worries forgotten. Hex continued, "The ogre went to sleep. At this point, an ordinary kid would be in big trouble. The door stood a hundred feet tall and was locked tight. Even getting off the table would be an impossible feat, because it towered five stories from the ground.

"Luckily, No Magic Girl was anything but ordinary." Hex leapt to her feet, dumping Queen Fuzzybutt III unceremoniously on the grass. She struck a heroic pose, her fists on her hips and chest puffed out. "'Impossible to use magic?' She scoffed. 'That doesn't matter to me!' Since she didn't have magic, she'd learned to rely on her bravery and wits. Instead of getting scared and crying, she looked around at her surroundings to see what she might use to escape."

Hex stalked across the yard, turning her head left and right like she was exploring a giant imaginary ogre's table. "No Magic Girl found dinner plates big enough to sleep on, cups so huge she could take a bath in them." Hex mimed scrubbing soap under her arms and Spanner laughed.

"On the other side of the table were some toothpicks half her height, a silk handkerchief the size of a blanket, and—" Hex took the coil of rope from the grass, "a piece of string as thick as her wrist." As she spoke, she tied one end of the rope to the tree at waist height, then picked up the ratty old scarf and threw it around her neck.

"No Magic Girl looked at the door. Just below an enormous doorknob was a keyhole taller than she was. For most people, these things wouldn't have seemed at all useful, but No Magic Girl was very clever. Do you know what she did then?"

Spanner shook his head, even though he knew exactly what she did then.

"She soaked one of the toothpicks in a huge cup of water, then bent it into a bow and used some silk thread from the handkerchief to make a bowstring." Hex found a fallen branch, bent it, and tied it with some of the string in her bag. It didn't look quite like the pictures she'd seen in history books about the tools ancient people used before they figured out how to control their magic with spells, but it would have to do. "No Magic Girl tied one end of the string to the cup and the other end to a broken toothpick. Then she shot the broken toothpick like an arrow, so it went right through the keyhole of the giant door."

Hex tied the rope to the end of a fallen twig, nocked her makeshift arrow, and aimed for a "V" where the tree trunk split in half. She pulled back and let go. The "arrow" didn't fly so much as wobble weakly and fall to the ground. Well, that wasn't entirely unexpected. She crossed the yard to the taller tree, dragging the stool behind her, then climbed up to the highest branch that could support her weight.

Then she realized she'd forgotten to bring the end of the rope up with her. Hex clenched her teeth to suppress a frustrated sigh. "Spanner, could you get the rope?"

Spanner nodded and carried the stick with the rope still tied to it until he was right below Hex. He laid it flat in his palms then commanded "*Levitate!*" and lifted both hands. The stick floated up slowly and leisurely as a bubble, trailing the rope below it.

A familiar pang of jealousy shot through Hex, followed immediately by guilt. Of course, she was glad Spanner could do magic and wasn't Undeveloped like she was. She swallowed her emotions, snatched the floating stick out of the air, and untied the rope from it.

"No Magic Girl pulled the rope to make sure the arrow caught crosswise against the keyhole." Hex tied the other end around the trunk so the rope stretched taut from where she sat in the branches back down to the other tree.

"Her rope-slide was ready. If she made a single mistake, she would fall to her death—but she'd have to take that risk to escape the ogre. No Magic Girl took a deep breath, held tightly and . . ."

Hex unwound the scarf from her neck and slung it over the rope to use as a handle. Spanner watched, his eyes shining with excitement. She wasn't sure if this would work—most of her projects didn't—but luckily for her, she wasn't actually trapped in an ogre cave. She braced herself to push off from the tree—

"Hey, look! It's the Mooch!"

Hex tensed at that word. It was an especially rude way of calling someone Undeveloped. As if she needed reminding of what a useless burden she was.

She craned out of the tree to see who had called her by that name. A large meaty boy and a small blonde girl strutted down the cobblestone road. She groaned. Gavaine and Morgaine—she knew them from school. They were always the first to start fights in class and to "accidentally" cast spells that would send smaller kids sprawling to the ground or make hair sprout from their noses.

Hex scrambled back down the tree, abandoning the rope-slide.

Queen Fuzzybutt III scuttled away as the two bullies shoved open the small gate to the yard.

"We heard you got kicked out of school because you're so stupid!" Gavaine guffawed.

Hex felt like she'd been slapped, like the bubble of stories and games she'd built over the summer had been popped and now reality was rushing back in. She had been a model student, excelling in every single one of her non-magical courses. But that hadn't mattered at the end of last year. The school's headmaster had told her parents politely but firmly that Undeveloped students couldn't continue because magic was required for the upper-level classes. It hadn't come as a surprise, but while Hex was still in school, she'd clung to a tiny shred of hope for a miracle. Even now, on the last day of summer break, Hex could hardly believe she wouldn't be going back to classes with everyone else tomorrow.

"Don't say mean things about my sister!" Spanner shouted.

"Don't you tell me what to do," Gavaine growled.

Hex stepped protectively in front of Spanner, but the bullies' attention had already moved on.

"What is *that*?" Morgaine jabbed a finger at the rope-slide. She had a vicious, goblin-like smirk on her face that put Hex on edge.

"None of your business," Hex snapped, but her cheeks burned.

"Oooh, the Mooch is trying to build one of her weird contraptions," Gavaine said, and to Hex's horror, he snatched her sketchbook from where it lay on the grass, still flopped open to the drawing of No Magic Girl escaping the ogre with her rope-slide. Hex grabbed for it, but Gavaine raised it over his head and out of her reach. "See, it's supposed to be this thing in the picture." He tossed the book to Morgaine.

"Hey, give it back!" Hex demanded.

"Go away!" Spanner chimed in. His usually sweet face was scrunched in anger—Hex hated seeing him that way.

Morgaine flipped through the book and screeched with laughter. *"No Magic Girl's Net-Trap? No Magic Girl's Water-Blaster?* What, are *you* supposed to be No Magic Girl?"

"No!" Hex's hand went to the beaded necklace around her neck. It was a simple thing, made of wooden alphabet beads that spelled NO MAJIK GURL. Spanner had given it to her for her birthday last year, and she never took it off. She shoved it under her shirt now. "They're just stories!"

"Uh-huh, *suuure.* And you build all this crummy stuff because you can't do magic." Morgaine waved the book at Hex.

"Give it back!" Hex yelled again and rushed at Morgaine.

Morgaine shoved the sketchbook under her arm, clapped her hands together, and pointed them at Hex. *"Stick!"* Hex couldn't stop fast enough—her left shoe magically stuck to the ground and she pitched forward. Her face smashed into the grass and the bullies whooped with high-pitched laughter.

"Hex!" Spanner cried, then shoved his hands at Morgaine. "*Push!*"

Morgaine stumbled back, releasing the Stick spell. Hex leapt to her feet and snatched the sketchbook from Morgaine, but Gavaine waved a lazy hand and uttered a spell that pulled the book right out of Hex's grasp and into his own. In the same instant, Morgaine regained her bearings and made a sharp tugging motion in Spanner's direction, crying, "*Pull!*" Spanner's legs flew out from under him and he landed in a heap.

"Spanner!" Hex shouted, running to him.

He had a scrape on one cheek and he blinked tears from his eyes, but he raised a hand and opened his mouth to cast a spell. Then he shot Hex a look of panic—he'd blanked out on whichever spell he'd been meaning to cast, like he often did when he was upset.

"Don't worry, Spanner," Hex said. Then she glared at Morgaine and Gavaine. "You cast another spell on my brother, and I'll—"

"You'll what?" Morgaine sneered. "You can't do anything—you're No Magic Girl!"

"I'm not—"

"No Magic Girl can do *anything!*" Spanner cut in, his face screwed in fury despite the tears streaking his cheeks.

"Oh yeah?" Gavaine said. "Then prove it!"

To Hex's horror, Spanner was already up on the stool and grabbing both ends of the scarf before she could stop him. She

hadn't tested the rope-slide yet to make sure it was safe for him!

"Spanner, don't—!"

He pushed off. For a breathless moment, Spanner slid. He actually slid, just like in her drawing!

Then there was a ripping sound, and the scarf forming the handle tore. Spanner toppled to the ground and his foot buckled under him, bent inward at an unnatural angle. For a second, everyone froze. Spanner gaped, too shocked to cry out. Then his face crumpled and he started to wail.

"Even your pathetic Mooch tricks don't work!" Morgaine shrieked with laughter. "Is there *anything* you're good at?"

"What a loser," Gavaine said. "Here, Mooch, you can have your lousy book back." He tossed it over his shoulder as he strolled off with Morgaine, the two of them still howling with laughter.

Hex didn't even look to see where it landed. She was already rushing toward her brother and rolling up the bottom of his pants. "Oh no, no, Spanner, let me see."

His small brown ankle was already swollen. Spanner was far too distraught to focus on a Heal spell, even if he could cast one powerful enough. Hex gently laid two fingers on his ankle. A glimmer of hope rose in her—maybe now that she really needed the magic, it would come to her. She closed her eyes so she could better recall the entry for Heal spells from *Spellman's Dictionary*, the large book in which every spell known to humankind was written.

"*Heal!*" she intoned, performing the incantation and the gesture specific to healing smaller injuries. Spanner sucked in a breath. Had it worked? Hex lifted her hand from his ankle to see if the swelling had disappeared.

It hadn't. Obviously. Hex pushed down her frustration and disappointment, and the ridiculous, ever-present hope that maybe *this* time the spell would work.

"Let's go inside and put some ice on it." Hex tried to sound like a responsible older sister, even though her throat felt tight. She'd had years to come to terms with being Undeveloped, years dealing with pitying looks from friends and feeling like a burden on her parents. But seeing her little brother suffer because of her and being unable to fix it? That was harder to handle.

Spanner nodded, still sobbing. Before he could push himself to his feet, Queen Fuzzybutt III slunk out from behind a bush with a plaintive meow. She nuzzled up to Spanner and started to shimmer an icy blue. Frost crackled across her body and the air around her grew cold. She nestled against his ankle like a big furry ice bag and Spanner exhaled in relief.

Great, even the cat is more useful than I am, Hex thought.

"Hex? Spanner! What's wrong?"

Hex looked up and saw their mother coming down the road for lunch. She broke into a run, with their father following closely behind.

"Oh, honey!" she said, kneeling by Spanner and laying a hand on his head.

"Some kids were being mean to me and Hex," Spanner sniffled. "They called her a Mooch."

"Hex Allen, don't you dare listen to those kids!" Her mom's face was torn between anger and concern. "You are my smart, kind, *amazing* daughter."

Hex turned her gaze to the floor and tried to squeeze back tears. A smart, kind, amazing daughter who was absolutely useless to everyone.

"Hex, you know how much we love you, right?" her father added. Still staring at the ground, she gave a small nod. He absentmindedly stroked her hair, smoothing down her dandelion puff of black curls. Hex poofed it back up. She was already the shortest kid her age. With the few inches of height her hair added . . . well, she was still the shortest, but at least she was short with *style*.

Her mother laid two fingers on Spanner's ankle. "*Heal!*" she intoned, using the same spell and gesture Hex had. But unlike Hex's attempt, it actually worked, and the swelling receded.

There was a metallic *ping* like a coin falling to the floor. Hex's mom lifted her hand. The slender thaumium ring on her forefinger that usually glowed a faint blue had faded to a dull silver.

"Phillip, the ring's just run out of magic. I'll need a new one," she said with a sigh.

Hex didn't miss the frown that flashed across her father's face before he patted her mother's arm and said, "Of course, Pozi dear."

Hex stared at the ground again, too ashamed to look into her parents' worried eyes. Thaumium charms like her mother's ring or her father's bangle amplified a person's magic. Most people wore some thaumium, since it was necessary to cast more powerful spells. Without it, the Heal spell could fix only minor cuts and bruises, but it took thaumium to fix something as big as a broken bone. But thaumium was expensive, and once its magic ran out, it was just ordinary, worthless metal. And now it was *Hex's* fault her mom had used up the last of the magic and would have to buy a new ring her family could barely afford. And the reason they could barely afford it? That was also Hex's fault.

She really *was* a Mooch. She wasn't going back to school tomorrow with everyone else and she would never find a real job because there weren't any jobs for Undeveloped people. Her parents would have to support her through adulthood, so they worked long hours at the apothecary and saved every spare penny. Hex tried to help them with their work, but since most of what they sold were potions for illnesses and diseases—which couldn't be cured with a simple spell—there was little she could do. The actual process of making the potions required magic, and she wouldn't earn them any more money just by helping with small tasks like running the front desk.

Maybe if she could fix this one thing—scrounge up just enough money to buy her mom a new thaumium ring—she could prove she wasn't entirely useless. Mr. Bobbin at the shop down the road sometimes hired kids part-time on weekends and during school breaks. He was always kind to her, even after she was diagnosed as Undeveloped. Maybe she could convince him to let her work despite her condition.

"Mom, Dad," Hex said, grabbing her bag that she'd left on the grass. "I need to take care of something in town. Can you take Spanner with you when you go back to the apothecary?"

"Of course, dear. What—"

But Hex was already running down the road.

WISHFUL THINKING

A bell tinkled as she entered Mr. Bobbin's store. It was a small building, taller than it was wide, with groceries like spicy cheese from fire goats, bread baked with butterfly butter, and dried jackalope meat stacked on shelves reaching twenty feet high.

Mr. Bobbin was hunched over the icebox, checking that the Freeze thaums were all still active. While raw thaumium was used to amplify magic, a thaum was enchanted to carry a single spell that could be turned on and off, saving the person the effort of having to continuously cast the spell. Like her mom's ring, thaums eventually ran out of magic, but Hex knew the real reason Mr. Bobbin checked the Freeze thaums was because sometimes kids turned them off as a prank. The last time that happened, a whole batch of ice fairy fruit melted all over the shop floor, leaving pools of silver glitter everywhere.

"Afternoon, Hex," he said, straightening up. "Wasn't your mother here just yesterday to buy groceries?"

"Yes, she was. Um, I didn't actually come for groceries . . . I wanted to ask you a question." Hex nervously spun the beads on her necklace. "Well, I won't be in . . ." Her next words felt glued to the inside of her throat and she had to force them out. "I won't be in school anymore. And I was wondering if maybe you need some help around the shop?" Mr. Bobbin's good-natured smile drooped, and a concerned crease formed between his brows. Hex added quickly, "It's okay if you pay me less because, I can't . . . you know . . . do magic . . ."

"Well, I'm not really looking for anyone right now . . ." He pointed at a girl stocking shelves in the back of the store. Hex recognized the girl's short brown hair—it was Belladonna. She and Hex had been close growing up. Hex couldn't remember quite why they'd drifted apart, since Belladonna was always nice to her.

"But Belladonna has to go back to school tomorrow. I can help instead!"

Mr. Bobbin avoided looking Hex in the eye, and her heart sank. It wasn't that he wasn't looking for anyone, it's that he wasn't looking for *her*. "Hex, I know you're a hard worker, but I need someone who can manage the high shelves, and turn the thaums on, and—"

"I—I can do some of that!" Hex cut in. "I know I can't turn the thaums on, but I can get stuff from the high shelves—watch." She pointed at the bread loaves on a shelf ten feet off the ground, which customers usually used a Slide or Fetch spell to get. After years of running grocery errands for her family, Hex was more than prepared.

She unslung her bag and pulled out some string and a bundle of sticks, each about a foot long. In a matter of minutes, she had lashed all the sticks together to form a much taller rod, and at the very end, she attached a hook. She maneuvered it so the hook was right at the corner of the bread—

"Hey, Hex! I thought I heard your voice," Belladonna said, strolling down the aisle. "Here, let me get that for you. *Slide!*" She pointed at the bread and flicked her wrist to the right. The bread slid off the shelf and fell directly into Belladonna's waiting hands.

An angry flush of heat flooded through Hex. "I could have gotten that."

"No, really—I'm always happy to help!" Belladonna said, handing Hex the bread. "I know it's hard for you being, um, you know . . . Undeveloped." She gave Hex the sort of sorrowful smile usually reserved for small injured animals.

Right, *that* was why they'd stopped being friends.

"Never mind," Hex muttered, too furious and mortified to meet their gazes. She practically threw the bread onto the counter and rushed out of the shop before either of them could respond.

Hex headed back up the road, her mind a storm of swirling, dark thoughts. How would she get her mom a new ring? And worse, how could she have a real life if no one believed she could do anything?

A few of Spanner's classmates ran past, laughing at the balls of colored lights they summoned from their hands. Hex felt a spurt of hot envy at how effortlessly they did magic. Tomorrow morning, Spanner and all the rest of them would go back to school while Hex . . . Hex didn't know *what* she'd be doing.

She was so wrapped up in her own head, she nearly walked into a small knot of people gathered around the town notice board. The daily newssheet had been posted and today's news drew a larger crowd than usual.

Hex stood on her tiptoes but was still too short to see over everyone's heads. "What's going on?" she asked Tristan, a teenager who lived a few houses over.

He stopped craning over the crowd to look at her. "You know the sandstorm over the Great Barren?"

Hex nodded. The Great Barren was an enormous desert toward the east, over the mountains. An eternal sandstorm raged over it, making it impossible to see. As if that wasn't bad enough, the desert was cursed—magic stopped working as soon as anyone set foot on its sands. The curse affected only humans, which meant that desert travelers were at the mercy of any dangerous creatures they encountered along the way. Most explorers who ventured into the desert never made it out again.

At the heart of it all was the Wishing Wyrm, an ancient dragon that lived in a volcano in the middle of the desert. Every hundred years or so, the sandstorm disappeared, opening a path to the dragon and the prize it offered: a single wish.

"Well," Tristan said, "the sandstorm's gone."

Hex didn't hear his next words. She was already weaving her way through the crowd, apologizing automatically as she stepped on someone's foot and accidentally elbowed one of her neighbors. The last time the sandstorm lifted was a hundred and seven years ago. Which meant one thing: she had a once-in-a-century chance to seize the wish that could make her normal.

3

A KNIGHT TO REMEMBER

Hex was breathless from running by the time she reached home. Her family was already gone—perfect. She dashed upstairs to her and Spanner's small room and threw open the curtains to let the light in since the Light thaums were all off. She pulled a large backpack from the cupboard. She'd rubbed wax all over its sturdy canvas surface after reading about how ancient people used wax to repel water before they'd discovered how to use thaums to sustain spells. Hex had read every single book about ancient people she could get her hands on. For ordinary people, the books were an interesting lesson in history. But for Hex, they were sources of information on how people managed basic tasks before they'd learned to harness magic or use thaumium. They were a treasure trove of solutions that made being Undeveloped a tiny bit less of a struggle.

She emptied out whatever junk she'd left in the backpack from the last time she'd used it, then threw in some clean clothes, a blanket, a small pouch of money her parents had given her for emergencies, her Thunder Knight fan club pin (for good luck), and her sketchbook. From her day bag, she transferred the tools she carried everywhere to make up for her lack of magic, including a small knife, rope, and some pieces of flint and steel—another trick used in ancient times.

Hex started to go downstairs to pack water and food, but stopped to look at the small room she shared with Spanner. She wanted to memorize their shared space, to capture a piece of it to recall on lonely nights. Her most treasured possessions were the hundreds of drawings adorning her walls. Many of them were of No Magic Girl's adventures and contraptions, or the Thunder Knight defeating his enemies, but Hex also drew anything else that sprang to mind. An entire corner was devoted to study of the human hand, another corner to the patterns of clouds and the wings of pixies. Spanner had contributed some drawings as well, mostly blobby stick figures of No Magic Girl or the Thunder Knight.

She turned to go, but her eyes landed on one of Spanner's drawings. He'd drawn the two of them as lumpy brown stick figures. Hex's hair was a mess of black scribbles and her left leg was inexplicably shorter than her right, while Spanner had given himself ears half the size of his head. Hex's eyes focused on the space in between the two figures where the stick arms connected, holding hands.

Hex touched her necklace. She couldn't just leave her family without a note. They'd be worried sick. And poor Spanner . . .

She tore a page out of her sketchbook and scribbled a letter.

Dear Mom, Dad, and Spanner,

I need to leave home for a little while to do something important. I'm sorry I won't tell you where I'm going, but please trust me when I say this is something I have to do. Please don't worry about me. I promise I'll be back.

Love,

Hex

P.S. Spanner, <u>paw</u>-lease don't forget to feed Queen Fuzzybutt III while I'm gone. She'll get <u>hiss</u>-terical if you <u>fur</u>-get.

Hex placed the letter on top of her pillow where it would be easy to find when her parents returned home in a few hours. She hoped they would forgive her.

She ran a hand over Spanner's drawing of the two of them, then sketched a heart just above their clasped hands. Her own heart ached as she turned away.

Less than a half hour later, Hex was on the cobbled road heading away from her hometown of Abrashire. She needed to walk only as far as Blinkenburgh, the next town over, and from there she could get a carriage ride directly to Midbar, the town at the edge of the Great Barren.

Shouts broke out, and Hex froze. Bandits and monsters were generally outside the towns, and she didn't think she'd be at risk in the middle of the day, this close to home. Better to be cautious, though. She climbed one of the steep grassy slopes that bookended either side of the road and crouched behind a bush where she still had a good view of the road. A woman riding a giant bear had a translucent blue Shield spell cast between her and a man in a Spin thaum-powered wagon.

"There's only one wish and it's mine!" the man screamed, throwing a fireball at the woman.

"No way!" The woman dropped the Shield spell and cast a Freeze spell. There was a burst of white-blue light, then frost grew from the man's chest and quickly spread over him, encasing his body. Underneath the layer of ice, his hands glowed orange, then burst alight as he melted himself out of his frozen shell.

Hex groaned. What was she thinking? *Everyone* was going after the wish. Why was she abandoning her family to go on some mad adventure when she hardly had a chance of succeeding? This wasn't one of her stories, this was *real life*.

At least for part of her journey, she'd have one small advantage—the others hunting the wish would find themselves without magic the moment they entered the Great Barren. Hex had an entire lifetime of practice doing things without magic, whereas they would have no idea how to cope. Their Spin thaum-powered wagons and Water spells would stop working, and who knew what monsters they'd have to face in the desert?

Some legends said the curse was like a storm and at the center, in the eye of the storm, the curse broke and magic was even stronger. But none of that mattered if the other wish hunters couldn't get that far. She had to beat them to the desert first, which would be—

BOOM!

Hex yelped as a clap of thunder and flash of lightning cut through the clear blue sky. She shook her head slightly and blinked a few times before realizing a muscular man atop a stormy gray horse had entered the fray. Little threads of lightning crackled across his hands.

No way. No sparking way. Hex's heart was in danger of thudding its way right out of her chest as she stared at that hawk-nosed, square-jawed face familiar from so many books and newssheets. His black and gold armor gleamed, and on his chest was the famous sigil—the thunderbolt symbol of the Thunder Knight.

"Thunder Knight! Thunder Knight!" The sound of trumpets and jubilant cheering reached Hex's ears and a mob of people flowed into the road. They carried banners and streamers, all emblazoned with his golden thunderbolt. Hex recognized people from not just Abrashire, but also the other neighboring towns. It seemed every single person in the entire valley had come to get a glimpse of the world-famous hero.

The Thunder Knight winked and blew a kiss to someone in the crowd. People screamed. One man swooned, an arm raised to his forehead. Hex felt a bit light-headed herself. How many of his stories had she read? How many of his adventures had inspired her own stories?

Then he turned and unleashed a glower on the quarreling wish hunters. The woman on the bear shrank back, and the man in the wagon gawked, a fireball still smoldering in one hand. "Fellow citizens of the kingdom," the Thunder Knight said, and the procession quieted at the sound of his deep voice. "Why this commotion? You're scaring the other travelers!"

The woman on the bear stared at the ground and mumbled something sheepishly.

"What was that?" the Thunder Knight boomed.

"He started it," she repeated in the same sulky voice Hex had heard Spanner use a thousand times.

"*Lightning!*"

Hex jumped as the sky boomed again and lightning flashed from the Thunder Knight's hands, leaving a scorched black scar in the middle of the road. No one could do a Lightning spell like the Thunder Knight. Most people got little more than a handful of sparks, but the Thunder Knight had honed the spell to a blast that could rival any thunderstorm. She'd heard he burned up an entire thaumium charm every time he used the spell.

"You will cease this nonsense! If you must fight, then take it off the roads. If you hurt a single innocent traveler, I will punish you ten times more harshly than I punished the troll army of the Griffin Pass—" He turned to face his procession, flashing a winning smile. "You know, when I saved the entire kingdom." The crowd roared in approval.

Hex knew she had a foolish grin plastered across her face, but she couldn't stop it. This was her chance! No one would dare attack the Thunder Knight. She could slip in with his entourage of admirers and parade in safety to Blinkenburgh. Maybe she'd even get a chance to meet the Thunder Knight himself and ask him about all his adventures! She'd definitely have to get him to autograph her sketchbook.

She stepped out from behind the bush, then froze as suddenly as if she'd been hit by a Stop spell. A petite woman with two severe black braids along her scalp pushed through the throng, her face twisted in concern.

"Mom!" Hex squeaked, then clapped a hand over her mouth. Her mother's voice was lost in the clamor but Hex recognized the shape her lips formed as her head whipped about frantically, searching: *Hex! Hex Allen!*

Hex shrank back. If only she hadn't left a note, she could have pretended she was there with the rest of the town to see the famous knight.

Her mother's anguished face tore at her. It wasn't too late. She could run out there now, give up this inane quest, and by evening she'd be home eating her mother's cream of jumping mushroom soup.

And then what? Continue living off her parents even into adulthood? Forever useless, forever regretting she'd had a shot at fixing things, but gave up before she even began? No. Going home wasn't an option. But neither was the safety of the Thunder Knight's retinue—her mom and half the town would drag her back home the moment they spotted her. She would have to manage on her own.

Hex took out her map and traced a finger over a path that ran parallel to the main road, but higher up in the mountain pastures. Following this path wouldn't add much time to her journey, but it would avoid any other wish hunters.

Hex sighed heavily and turned her back on her hero and her mother. She had a dragon to find.

ON THE MOOOVE

Hex tromped her way up one of the many well-trodden paths to the mountain pastures, trying to come up with a plan. Would a carriage from Blinkenburgh be fast enough to beat the other wish hunters? And what would she do when she arrived at the Great Barren? She still needed a way—

"Yikes!" Hex stumbled over something small and soft. A calf stared back up at her, its dark eyes wide and doleful.

"Oh no! I'm so sorry, little guy!" Hex dropped to her knees. It didn't look hurt, just startled. It mooed at her pitifully and she stroked its head.

She realized her mistake a few seconds too late when she heard a much louder moo behind her. Hex turned to stare into the face of a very angry-looking cow.

"And I guess that's your mama," Hex said, standing up slowly. She backed away from the calf, trying not to make any sudden movements. The mama cow huffed, and a small tongue of flame shot out of its mouth.

Great. She couldn't have made just any cow angry, it had to be a fire-breathing cow. Hex continued retreating as slowly as possible. She was six feet away, then seven. The cow didn't follow, but it stared at Hex, pawing the ground threateningly.

Hex's heel hit a rock and she stumbled backward with a strangled shout. The cow bellowed monstrously, spewing flames, and charged. Hex scrambled to her feet and ran. She could feel the heat of the fire on her neck. She glanced over her shoulder and yelped. The cow was gaining on her. "*Sleep!*" she shouted, pointing over her shoulder and making a tipping motion with her hand. Nothing happened. What did she expect? If she were normal, she wouldn't be on this ridiculous quest in the first place.

In her stories, No Magic Girl would have stumbled across an oh-so-convenient pile of materials. She'd have an epiphany about what to make. *And* the cow would suddenly become distracted, giving her plenty of time to put it all together.

Sparks! No Magic Girl had it easy!

She thought she heard a growl buried under the sounds of the hoofbeats and whooshing of flames. She grimaced. What other dangerous creatures were lurking nearby? It wouldn't help to escape being fried by the cow if she ran into the jaws of an angry porcubear.

The growl grew into a roar. Hex spared another look over

her shoulder and gaped. A boy hurtled across the ground in a strange-looking metal cart, a large pair of blue-tinted goggles all but obscuring his face. The cart barreled down the dirt path at incredible speed, leaping in the air every time it hit a bump or rock. He caught up to the cow, then rode right past it until he was just ahead of Hex, grinning like mad the entire time.

"Jump on!" he shouted.

Hex screamed and made a flying leap onto the cart, grabbing the boy's shoulders and nearly pulling him off.

"Ha ha!" he yelled, punching the air. Hex glanced back to see the cow losing ground as they flew headlong toward a copse of trees.

"You'll have to *mooove* faster than that, cow!" Hex shouted. She half expected the boy to groan—people (other than Spanner) usually did when she made a pun—but she thought she saw his smile widen.

There was a loud *ker-thunk* as one of the wheels caught on a tree root, and the next thing she knew, Hex was flying through the air. She landed heavily on her side and scrambled back to her feet immediately. The cow was charging toward them, and her rescuer was sprawled on the ground, looking dazed.

"Come on, come on, come on!" Hex grabbed his wrist and ran for a nearby tree, yanking him behind her. She clambered up easily, but the boy didn't follow. He was wobbling back and forth, still disoriented from the fall. Hex bit her lip, then dropped back down and helped him climb to a large branch halfway up the tree.

WHAM! Hex yelped as the cow slammed into the tree, shaking it from trunk to tip.

"Holy cow! Lucky it can't climb, huh?" the boy said, smiling a little dizzily at Hex. The cow glowered up at them, then belched a stream of fire. The dry leaves on the lowest branch began to smolder and his smile fell. "Uh-oh, that's not good."

"Cast a Sleep spell!" Hex shouted at him. "Or a Stick spell on its feet! Anything!"

"I can't!" he wailed.

"What?" Hex blinked. The boy's dazed smile had given way to wide-eyed panic. Maybe he was too scared to focus on casting the spell, like Spanner when he was upset.

The cow paced angrily below them, spitting out balls of flame. The smoke was getting thick enough to make breathing difficult.

"What do we do?" the boy coughed.

How was she supposed to know? It wasn't often she was stuck in a tree with an angry fire-breathing cow trying to trample her. She yanked off her shoe and threw it at the cow as hard as she could. It hit the cow between the ears and bounced off. The cow didn't even flinch.

Hex racked her brain. The Thunder Knight would scare off the cow with a blast of lightning, but obviously that wasn't an option. She was thinking about this all wrong. What would No Magic Girl do?

A few weeks ago, she'd told Spanner a story about No Magic Girl defeating a shadow wolf. In the story, No Magic Girl used a stretchy cord tied to a forked piece of wood to launch a rock into the wolf's eye. Hex and Spanner had spent the next day making their own versions to throw small pebbles across the yard—one of her few projects that had actually worked in real life. It wasn't the best plan, just another one of her stories, but Hex couldn't think of anything else.

She dug through her backpack, then moaned. "I didn't pack the stretchy cord!"

"Stretchy cord? I think I've got something like that!" The boy patted down his lime green vest, which was covered in pockets overflowing with metal objects, wires, and string. He dumped a curious assortment of oddities into a hollow in the branch—a silver cylinder with wires sprouting out, a metal tool with a thin handle and gaping jaws, several coin-shaped objects, and a piece of ribbon with numbers written on it.

"Aha!" The boy flourished a length of thick, rubbery cord. "What's it for?"

"I'm going to tie it to a forked stick and use it to launch something at the cow," Hex said.

"Like a slingshot, you mean?" He made a "V" with his two fingers and mimed pulling back a cord—exactly like what Hex and Spanner had made.

"Yes, a slingshot!" Hex had never heard the word *slingshot*, but she liked it. She took the cord from the boy and gave it an experimental pull. It was thicker and longer than the cord she used with Spanner, which gave her an idea: if she could use a forked branch for a small slingshot, why not use the entire tree to make a huge one? Small pebbles wouldn't faze the cow, but a bigger slingshot meant bigger projectiles.

But what would they launch at the cow? It had barely noticed the shoe, although the slingshot would let her shoot it a lot harder. They needed to do something to make it stop breathing fire.

"If there was some way we could use the slingshot to throw water at it . . ." she mused.

The boy snapped up several small, colorful sacks from the pile. "What about water balloons?"

"Water baboons?"

"Oh, right. Um, it's like a small Bubble spell, kind of, and you can fill it with water. Here, I'll show you. Can I have your water flask?"

Hex passed him the flask, and while he filled a balloon, she grabbed a funnel from the pile. She used her knife to cut four holes, one pair on each side of the funnel. Then, she cut the rubbery cord in two and threaded each piece through a pair of the holes. She tied both of them into loops about the length of her arm, slinging one of the cords around a tree branch before knotting it.

Below them, the cow spit out another ball of flame. Hex and the boy both screamed in unison as it flew past the tree, just barely missing them.

The boy passed her the water balloon, his hands still shaking, and Hex almost dropped it in surprise. It was squishy! She could feel the water sloshing around inside, deforming the balloon as she squeezed it. "How will the water get out?"

"Like a Bubble spell popping," the boy said.

Hex wasn't entirely sure what to expect, but she handed the boy the other end of the rubbery cord. "Hold tight," she said. With the cord looped around the tree branch on one side and the boy gripping it on the other, she'd rigged together a giant slingshot. She placed the water balloon into the funnel and pulled it back as far as she could.

"Eat this, you big *COW-ard*!" she shouted and let go. The cords snapped forward with such force the balloon flew into the mouth of the astonished cow. It exploded on impact, water gushing from the cow's muzzle. Hex gaped. What kind of magic *was* this?

The cow looked as stunned as Hex felt. Then it bellowed in anger and tried to let loose another blazing breath. Instead, a pathetic trickle of smoke dribbled out.

Hex grabbed the boy's arm and leapt down from the tree, avoiding the branches where the dry leaves had caught alight. The cow was still frozen with shock and didn't follow when they ran

down the hillside. They kept running—with Hex trying to ignore every rock and branch jabbing into her shoeless foot—until they were sure they'd lost the cow. The boy collapsed against a tree trunk, half panting and half laughing.

"That was nuts and bolts!" the boy said. He pushed his goggles back into coils of black hair, revealing chestnut brown cheeks and round eyes crinkled from a lopsided smile.

"Yeah, that was nearly a *cow-tastrophe*!" Hex replied.

"That cow had a real *beef* with you!"

"Ouch, I should've let the cow barbecue you," Hex said, "because you're so *cheesy*!"

"You've got to stop *milking* the same joke," he replied, grinning at her.

"I thought my joke was *udderly* brilliant!"

He wavered, his brow furrowed in thought. "I . . . can't think of a clever response," the boy conceded.

"Are you all *burned* out?" Hex said before she could stop herself.

He looked at her with an expression of utmost admiration. "You're good. Ace job with that water balloon trick! I'm Cam," he said, standing up and shaking her hand energetically.

Because she was on the small side, Hex was surprised the boy was not much taller than her. He looked her age, or maybe a little older. And he was covered in soot marks from head to toe. Hex looked down at her own bright blue dress and was dismayed to find it looked just as bad. At least her backpack had made it through the incident in one piece.

"I'm Hex," she said. "Lucky you had those balloon things!"

"Oh, I've got loads! Take some." He shoved a few brightly colored ones into her hand. "They're a lot of fun!"

"Thanks," Hex said, stuffing them into her backpack. "Sorry about your cart . . . If that cow's gone, we can go back and get it. Maybe it'll be fixable."

"That'd be great! We can get your shoe back too!" Cam said, trotting back in the direction they'd come from. "Thanks for saving us."

"Well, I would have been a flambéed pancake if you hadn't shown up," Hex said. "What're you doing up here anyway?"

"My friend and I are traveling on the main road. I climbed up the hill to, um, you know . . ." He shrugged shyly. "To pee. I saw you off in the distance being chased, so I grabbed my go-cart and came to help."

"Won't your friend be worried about you?" Hex asked.

"Nah, she won't worry. She knows I can take care of myself okay. I told her I'd catch up," Cam replied as they approached the tree.

Several of the leaves still smoldered but the fire was already dying. Fortunately, the cow was gone. Hex found her shoe nestled in the roots, slightly singed and very squashed. She retrieved the rubber cord from the giant slingshot and gave it back to Cam.

Hex was about to ask which direction Cam was going when they reached his—what had he called it?—go-cart. It was mostly intact, although the front was crumpled from where it had hit the tree root. Cam prodded it, pushing and turning various buttons and knobs. He shrugged. "Well, it's not working. I'll haul it back and fix it later." He took a short length of rope from his pocket and tied it to the go-cart.

"Maybe the Spin thaums got dislodged?" Hex suggested.

"The Spin thaums . . . ?" Cam asked. "Oh . . . it doesn't use Spin thaums."

"Then how does it move? A Push thaum? Slide?" She scanned the ground for the metallic gleam of thaumium.

"Naw, none of those thaum things. It works without magic."

Hex stopped searching and stared at Cam, trying to figure out if he was joking. His face radiated sincerity. "What do you mean, it works without magic?"

"Um. Well . . ." He bounced on the balls of his feet, brimming with a sort of restless energy.

Hex remembered the comment he'd made in the tree. "Wait a second, you also . . . you can't—" She hesitated. There was no way . . . "You weren't just panicking when you said you couldn't cast any spells?"

"Well, I *was* panicking," Cam admitted, "but that's right. I can't do magic. And . . . neither can you, right?"

"You mean . . . you're Undeveloped too?" Hex had never met anyone else Undeveloped before. "Wait—no, that can't be right. There's no way a cart can go that fast without magic. Are you just messing with me? Because it's not funny."

"No, I really can't do magic. Look," Cam said. He held out his left hand, and she saw he was wearing a thaumium ring.

Cam waved his hand in the familiar gesture of the basic Light spell and said "*Light!*" Nothing happened. No sparks, no burst of light. Only someone completely unable to use magic—someone Undeveloped—could try to cast a spell with the aid of thaumium and have absolutely nothing happen. Hex knew all too well from personal experience. "It used to be my mom's. I keep it as a memento," he said, with a slightly sheepish grin, "but it's useless to me."

Hex was stunned. "You didn't use magic to build that go-cart?"

Cam shook his head. To her surprise, he was smiling unabashedly now. What sort of person was *proud* to be Undeveloped? "Not a lick!"

"Then how *did* you make it?"

"I . . . don't think I'm supposed to tell people about it." He drummed his fingers nervously on his leg. "But . . . what you did with that slingshot was awesome. Makes me think you'd be really good at it."

"Really good at what?" Hex demanded.

Cam smiled an enormous, toothy grin, his eyes sparkling. "Clank."

5

CLANK YOU VERY MUCH

"Clank?" Hex repeated. "Like the sound a pan makes when you drop it?"

"Or when you hammer something metal, or two robots collide, or your gear train isn't aligned right." Cam sighed dreamily. What was he *talking* about? He looked at Hex and blinked. "Um, I didn't expect you to understand any of that . . . got a bit carried away there. Which direction are you going?"

"That way." Hex pointed down the path she'd been following.

"Perfect, I'm going in the same direction! I can explain along the way." They began trudging down the hill, Cam hauling the go-cart behind him.

"So, what's clank?" Hex pressed.

Cam's brow scrunched, and his lower lip jutted out in an expression of almost comical thoughtfulness. "You know, it's funny, I haven't figured out a good way to explain it." When he finally spoke, he let each word roll off his tongue slowly and carefully.

"Well, magic isn't the only law of nature that makes things work. Clank is . . . clank is the things we make by understanding those other laws, instead of using magic. You already know some of it even if you don't realize it—like when you pulled on the slingshot, you knew it would spring back and launch the balloon."

"There's nothing special about knowing that. It's just how things work," Hex said. "It doesn't explain how you built your go-cart to move uphill without magic."

"But it does! See, once you know some of those laws of nature— call 'em science for now—you can use them to build clank! It takes a creativity most normal people don't have, because they're so used to relying on magic. They can only cast the spells in *Spellman's Dictionary*, but clank isn't limited by anything—'cept the laws of nature and your imagination."

He fell silent, and Hex thought about her notebook full of sketches of all the things No Magic Girl made on her adventures. The rope-slide, the slingshot, fire using flint and steel to make a spark instead of using an incantation, or using a tarp and sticks to build a shelter. She'd never actually built most of her designs, but even just in her imagination she tried to think through how they might actually work. No one else she knew bothered thinking about those kinds of designs because they didn't need them. If they wanted to stay warm, they'd use a Heat or Flame spell; if they wanted shelter, they'd cast a Shield spell against the rain.

Hex stopped and retrieved her sketchbook from her backpack, then stiffened, remembering the cruel words and shrieks of laughter from Gavaine and Morgaine.

Cam waited for her, smiling in a good-natured way at nothing in particular. She'd only just met him, but for reasons she couldn't understand herself, she handed him the sketchbook. "Are you telling me the stuff in here is clank?"

Cam opened the notebook. Hex fidgeted with her necklace. Compared to his clank go-cart, her drawings seemed childish, and she had to fight the urge to grab the sketchbook back. He turned to the next page, and then the next, his lopsided smile gradually growing wider and wider. "Holy helical lock washer," he said, finally looking up at her. His eyes were blazing. "This is incredible! You came up with all this stuff yourself?"

Hex's cheeks grew warm, but she couldn't help smiling a little. "They're . . . they're just drawings for stories I tell my little brother." She took the sketchbook back.

"Wow, your little brother is a lot luckier than mine!" His smile faltered. "I wish I could draw stuff like that for him."

"You're not good at drawing?" Hex asked.

"Absolutely awful," he admitted.

"Well, they're just sketches, anyway. I haven't actually made most of the stuff in real life," Hex said, feeling self-conscious but oddly buoyant at the same time. "I'm sure most of it wouldn't even work."

Cam frowned, like he wanted to say something. Then he brightened. "Come eat dinner with us! I can tell you more about clank, and you can meet my friend." He started walking again with a cheerful bounce in his step. "She's a Clanksmith, like I am. Like you could be—you're a natural!"

Hex's first instinct was to say no. She couldn't waste time if she wanted to beat the other wish hunters to the Wyrm. But she'd need to stop for food anyway, and a hot dinner sounded nice. "Sure, but I can't stay for long. How did you learn this . . . this clank stuff anyway? I've never heard of it before."

"Well, we usually keep it a secret these days. But it wasn't always that way. Before people learned to control magic, they made clank. Then they learned how to cast spells and they used clank a little bit less. And a while after that, thaumium was discovered and kinda changed everything. Thaumium made it much easier to do more powerful magic and to store spells. Can you imagine how a wagon would work if you couldn't just attach some Spin thaums?" Hex didn't have to imagine—she'd seen it herself. Spanner had a small toy cart he would send racing around the yard with a Spin spell, twirling his fingers until his hands were tired and he felt light-headed from using so much magic. She wasn't even sure it was possible to propel a full-size wagon *without* thaumium. "Eventually, normal people stopped using clank because magic was so much easier, until only Undeveloped people made clank."

"So, how come I never read about clank in the history books?"

"Because people forgot about it and erased it from history. Mostly. Did your history books talk about how ancient people made bows and arrows or plows?" Hex nodded. "That's clank. It's simple clank—but so are wheels and metal and things people still use today that no one would think of as clank."

"Then why is it secret?"

"Well . . . when people stopped understanding clank, they got suspicious and scared of it. It was even outlawed in some places, hundreds of years ago, and Clanksmiths were forced to hide. I mean . . . clank *can* be dangerous. Bad people can use it to make weapons scarier than anything you can do with magic. But really, I think it's just that people get scared of what they don't understand. So now we keep it secret, or pretend it's magic. Like my go-cart— everyone just thinks it uses Spin thaums."

"But your go-cart is noisier than if it had Spin thaums," Hex said.

"Yeah, but you assumed it used Spin thaums anyway. People don't recognize clank anymore, so they just assume it must be magic," Cam pointed out. He was right—it had never occurred to Hex that his go-cart might be anything *other* than magic. If he'd told her the Spin thaums were just broken and that's why they were so noisy, she would have believed him, even though that wasn't how thaums worked.

"If clank is so secret . . . why are you telling me about it?"

"Because I think every Undeveloped person has the right to know about clank." Cam's mouth was set in a determined line, and for a moment his words had an almost physical weight to them.

The road came into view as they descended into the valley. Parked just off to the side was a bizarre-looking carriage. At first glance, it looked like a fairly standard open-sided coach, but it had two round glass panels in front where there were normally Light thaums. The driver's seat had a wheel and several knobs and levers instead of the usual two pieces of thaumium that activated the right and left Spin thaums. The most distinctive part was the fabric canopy, which was covered in some kind of bluish-black glass that gleamed in the sunlight.

Cam followed Hex's gaze, then perked up. Well, perked up even *more*. "That's our car!" he said. "Fuse should be nearby!"

He scrambled down the slope, with the go-cart bouncing behind him, and Hex followed. Fortunately, there weren't any wish hunters around. Cam stopped when they reached the carriage—or car, as he called it—by the road. "Can you help me load the go-cart?"

"Sure." Hex knelt by one end of the go-cart and raised it up. She gasped and almost stumbled—it was a lot heavier than it looked. "What is this thing made of?"

"Oh yeah, sorry. The battery and the motor weigh a lot." Cam grunted as he lifted and his next words came out strained. "Those

47

are more clank, I can explain later." Together, they managed to heave the go-cart into the large cargo space in the back of the car. Cam climbed aboard, then rummaged through a large metal chest wedged between the go-cart and the back of the seats before emerging with a book and a small tin box.

"Here, take a look at this during dinner," he said. "It's an intro to clank—I think you'll really like it! The box has a bunch of beginner stuff you can try—batteries, some small motors, LEDs—those are kind of like Light thaums. It's all explained in the book."

The book was a heavy tome that had clearly been well-used and abused. Despite that, it was beautiful, with its brown leather cover adorned with intricate carvings and the title inlaid in gleaming brass letters: *The Curious Book of Clank*.

Even as Hex accepted the book, Morgaine's words rang in her head: *Even your pathetic Mooch tricks don't work! Is there* anything *you're good at?*

Cam's enthusiasm had kept her doubts briefly at bay, but they rushed back all at once. Drawing pictures and telling stories were one thing, but the chasm between that and making something like Cam's go-cart seemed impossibly wide. What if it was like school all over again? She'd memorized the incantations and perfected the gestures, but when it came time to perform, she couldn't muster even a spark of magic. What was the point in getting her hopes up only to find out she was just as bad at clank as she was at magic?

"Um, thanks. I'll take a look later." She put the book and the box into her backpack. "Where's your friend?"

"Up there!" Cam pointed up the hill opposite to the one they'd come down. Behind a bush, Hex could just make out the flickering of a fire. She followed Cam and was surprised when she finally saw the unusual source of the fire. A small metal canister contained the flames, and there was no sign of a Fire thaum or wood and smoke.

If the campfire was strange, it was nothing compared to the person sitting in front of it. She was lean and long, with an olive complexion and goggles perched in short spiky hair enchanted to a vivid turquoise. Like Cam, her overalls were covered from top to bottom in pockets, each one stuffed with a small glass vial or pouch. As Hex watched, the girl put the end of a long, thin stick into the fire, her dark eyes glittering with mischief. Hex gaped as the end of the stick sparked, then burst into bright light, like a shooting star. Then it fizzled into nothing, leaving just a bright afterimage.

"You're back!" the girl said, tossing the stump of stick into the fire.

"Fuse, this is Hex!" Cam announced.

Fuse glanced at Hex and frowned. "You brought someone with you? Cam, we don't got time for that, we gotta keep moving." She handed Cam a sausage from a pan along with a piece of bread, then turned a knob on the metal canister and the fire went out. Hex eyed the canister with suspicion, wondering if there was actually a Fire thaum inside. "Come on, you can eat while I drive."

"Hex is going in the same direction, so we can talk on the way," Cam said. He folded the bread around the sausage then tore the whole thing in two and gave Hex half. It was greasy and delicious. "You'll like her! She built a giant slingshot! And . . ." He lowered his voice, even though they were a good distance from the road. "She's like us."

"She blows things up for fun?" the girl suggested, raising a sparse black eyebrow. It looked like it was missing patches, and . . . were those burn marks on her overalls?

"No," Cam said, oblivious to the sarcasm. "She's Undeveloped also, so—"

"You too?" Hex exclaimed, gawking at Fuse. "But your hair and those sparks and—"

"Clank," Cam and Fuse said in unison.

"All right, okay," Fuse said. "Just get in the car so we can keep moving, and you can convince me on the way why I shouldn't just kick Hox—"

"Hex."

"—into the road."

"Fuse isn't serious," Cam said, although Fuse smirked a little too devilishly for Hex's comfort. "Come on, ride with us for a bit. We can drop you off somewhere farther down the road. I'll tell you more about clank on the way!" He clambered into the back seat of the car and Hex followed.

"Cam, you know you're not supposed to just go around telling everyone about clank, right?" Fuse hopped into the driver's seat and pulled one of the strange levers. The car made a growling sound like Cam's small go-cart. Hex started as it surged forward faster than any carriage she'd ever ridden in.

"I don't tell everyone!" Cam protested. "I told her because she'd make a great Clanksmith!"

Fuse let out a beleaguered sigh and turned to Hex. "So, what's your story?"

"Uh, well, I was getting chased by this fire-breathing cow—"

"Right, *why* were you getting chased by a fire-breathing cow?"

"I tripped over its calf and it got angry. It was a *mis-steak*." Hex grinned at the pun, but Fuse just groaned.

"I thought you were *pasture* cow puns," Cam added.

"Don't encourage her!" Fuse said.

"Anyway, I was coming from Abrashire," Hex continued. "You probably passed it on the road."

"Where're you going?"

Hex opened her mouth, then snapped it shut.

"Yeah, you never did say where you're going!" Cam added.

They were going in the same direction as her, and Fuse seemed to be very concerned about moving quickly. And they were Undeveloped, like her . . .

Realization struck like a Thunder Knight lightning bolt. They were also after the Wyrm.

Typical of her rotten luck to finally meet other kids who were Undeveloped like her, and to have them be her rivals. She didn't know how or why Cam and Fuse agreed to cooperate with each other—according to the legend, the Wyrm would only allow the wish to be used on a single person. Even if they got the wish, one of them would remain Undeveloped. Whatever their deal was, she was another rival and she'd seen for herself how the wish hunters treated each other.

She decided her best option was to keep quiet and leave them at the first chance when it didn't seem suspicious. "Um. I'm going to visit my . . . uncle." She waved a hand vaguely toward the road. "He lives in Blinkenburgh."

Fuse's eyes narrowed. "And your parents just sent you by yourself, on monster- and bandit-infested roads? I'm an orphan so I'm no expert, but that seems like bad parenting." She tapped her nose thoughtfully. "Big backpack, obviously lying about where you're going . . . you're running away, aren't you?"

"Yes!" Hex said, and then realized she sounded too relieved. "I mean, oh no, you caught me. I'm running away!"

"Oh no! Why are you running away?" Cam asked.

"It's my parents . . . because I'm . . . you know, Undeveloped." The lie jabbed like a needle in her heart. It was a good lie—she knew very well that many parents abandoned their Undeveloped children. She was extremely lucky to have loving parents, and it felt like a betrayal to pretend otherwise.

Cam's eyebrows drew together. "I'm sorry. I understand . . . my dad left me at an orphanage when I was little."

Hot guilt trickled through Hex. She was lying to someone who had it much worse than she did.

"Well, if you don't have anywhere you're running to, you want to travel with us?" Cam asked. "We can teach you clank on the way!"

Hex gulped. "Um, I couldn't possibly—I mean, there's no way we're headed in the same direction."

"But . . . you just said you're running away. Does it matter where you're going?" Cam asked.

Her lie was unraveling with every earnest question from Cam. She struggled to recover. "Well, I sort of wanted to go to a big city like Runemont . . ."

"Oh . . . that's kind of the opposite direction of where we're going. We're going east, to the Wishing Wyrm."

"Cam!" Fuse slapped her forehead with her palm. "You're not supposed to tell people that!"

"Oh yeah, but she's our friend now, so I figured—"

"You just met her! She's not our friend—no offense, Hex," Fuse said, flashing Hex a quicksilver grin. The grin froze and then slid off her face.

"Wait a second. Big backpack, obviously lying about where you're going . . . You're not running away—you're after the Wyrm too, aren't you?"

Hex made a strangled humming sound in the back of her throat as she tried to think of another lie and failed. "Uh. Yeah. I am."

Cam's face fell. " . . . Does that mean we can't be friends?"

"Yes, Cam, that is exactly what that means," Fuse said, rolling her eyes.

Hex bit her lip. She liked Cam, and clank seemed interesting enough. But this was a competition, and Hex wouldn't let anything stand in her way. "It was nice meeting you," she said. "You can drop me off anywhere, seeing as we're—um, well, you know." She was about to say "enemies" but that seemed too harsh.

"Yep, nice meeting you, bye!" Fuse stopped the car.

"Wait a sec—" Cam protested. "It's almost dark. Can't she stay with us just for the night?"

"Cam, she's our *rival*," Fuse said. "She's lucky we're just letting her go and not tying her up and leaving her for the monsters."

"Hey!" Hex protested.

"We can't all be as nice as Cam," Fuse shrugged.

"Well, thanks for saving me earlier, Cam," Hex said as she clambered out of the car. "Good lu—" She paused. What was she thinking? *Good luck*? Cam was nice, but that wish was *hers*. "May the best person win," she corrected herself.

The car roared down the road, leaving Hex by herself. Even though the road was empty, she hiked back up the hills just to be safe. It was getting dark, and Hex knew she'd have to find a place to camp soon. She didn't like the idea of stopping—since Cam and

Fuse could take turns sleeping, they could continue their journey long through the night. And unlike the rest of the wish hunters, the desert's curse wouldn't slow them down at all. She had to get to Blinkenburgh to get a carriage if she had any shot at keeping up.

When she couldn't see more than a few feet in front of her, she pulled the flint and steel from her backpack and scrounged under a nearby bush until she found a dry branch to set alight. The branch provided some light and warmth, but it was burning so quickly it wouldn't last long. Hex couldn't help but shiver. She was hardly a day out of Abrashire . . . but there had been rumors of rock trolls and other monsters coming down from the Troublesome Mountains at night, in search of tasty humans who might be wandering the road and surrounding areas. And what about Shades? Her stomach fluttered just thinking about it and she had to remind herself that no one even knew if they really existed.

She staggered on, even as the waxing moon arced slowly across the sky and her head filled with cotton and her eyelids dragged down. She couldn't sleep; she had to get to the Wyrm. But when her branch burned out, she stumbled and fell onto the grass. She needed to sleep. Just a little nap and then she could keep going, refreshed.

Hex spread out her blanket. As her eyes sank closed, she remembered she still had Cam's book and box of clank in her backpack. Oh well. They were rivals now anyway.

Hex didn't know how long she'd been asleep when something suddenly squeezed her torso. She didn't even get a chance to cry out before a blow to her head made everything go dark.

6

A BRIGHT IDEA

Hex's eyes fluttered open. It was dark—was it still nighttime? Her head throbbed, and she tried to rub her temples but she couldn't move her arm above her elbow. She gasped—something was pinning her arms to her sides! As her eyes adjusted, she saw a rope was wrapped around her biceps and torso, and another around her legs. Where in the world was she?

She looked up, and instead of stars she saw the faint outlines of long, pointy stalactites. She looked down—she was tied to a giant wooden chair half the height of her house. Directly in front of her was a table bigger than her room at home with a fancy rug underneath. In the dim light, she could make out a gigantic shelf full of books on the other side of the cave. A coat rack as tall as a sapling was next to an even taller wooden door. Whatever lived here was big. Monstrously big. What creature that big owned *furniture*?

A memory of her own voice floated through her head. *But barely a mile outside of town, what did No Magic Girl encounter?*

Oh no.

A sleeping ogre!

Oh no no no.

Hex fought back a wave of panic as she surveyed her surroundings. It wasn't like her stories. There was no pile of materials lying around to be turned into a rope-slide, no Hex-sized keyhole in the door for her to escape through.

Even if there had been a keyhole, she wouldn't have fit through it. In her stories, ogres towered a hundred feet tall and could crush humans like bugs between their fingers. But the chair she was tied to belonged to a creature that couldn't have been more than four or five times her height. Unfortunately, that was still four or five times larger than any creature she'd like to fight, armed with nothing but her (currently tied-up) bare fists. Her backpack with her supplies was nowhere to be seen.

"Oh, you're awake!" rumbled a voice from the other end of the cave. Hex squinted in the gloom, and what she'd taken for a shadowy recess resolved itself into a large figure. The ogre—or ogress, Hex guessed, based on the elaborate hairdo and glittery velvet dress—crossed the room in several long strides and crouched before Hex. "Excellent! I was starting to worry I'd hit you too hard."

"Does it matter, if you're just going to kill me and eat me anyway?" Hex said, trying to sound brave despite the huge face looming in front of her. The ogress wasn't as ugly as Hex had imagined in her stories. Her features weren't entirely human—they were broader and thicker, and from what Hex could tell in the low light, her skin had a gray cast to it. Hex's eyes gravitated down toward the ogress' teeth, each one the size of Hex's fist, and she shuddered.

The ogress stared at Hex for a moment, her jaw slack. "You—you think I'm going to *eat* you?" She sounded utterly disgusted.

"Isn't that why you kidnapped me?" Hex asked.

"I'm a pescatarian!"

"You . . . only eat pesky people?"

"Fish! I only eat fish! I'd never eat human—you're full of all kinds of nasty contaminants and neurotoxins!" The ogress huffed. "Let's start this again. My name is Grundzilla, and I kidnapped you because I need your magic."

Hex hesitated. She'd been so certain the ogress was going to eat her that her brain needed a moment to reconfigure. "Come again?"

"Well, ogres can't do magic, which is sparking inconvenient—you wouldn't know, being human and all." Hex almost interrupted to say actually, *yes*, she did know about the inconvenience of not being able to do magic, but decided to keep that information to herself. "And really, I don't need magic *most* of the time. But there's a few chores and other things that would be great to have magic for. Like, one thing that *really* bothers me is reading at night!"

"You need magic to read books?"

"No, I need *light* to read books!" Grundzilla rolled her eyes as though an ogress needing a reading light was the most obvious thing in the world. "We ogres have excellent night vision, of course, but even we can't read in the dark."

The only light in the cave came from a small, flickering flame. It took Hex a moment to figure out it was a candle, something ancient people used. It was a lot dimmer than the cool white glow of a Light thaum. "What's wrong with using your candle to read?"

"You think I haven't tried?" Grundzilla pounded a fist on the table. "I keep burning the edges of pages or dripping wax on the book. And then I have to light the darn thing. You humans, you snap your fingers, say a spell, and *voilà*! You have light. But for me, I have to sit there with some flint or try to catch a fire salamander to get a flame going. And the *worst* is when the light goes out unexpectedly!" The ogress threw her arms up in exasperation. "Just last week, I was reading *The Amorous Adventures of Amalda the Alchemist: Book Two, The Vampyre Prynce*, and just when the prynce was *finally* about to kiss Amalda, I sneezed and blew my candle out!"

"Sounds like the candle was trying to get back *achoo*." The pun slipped out before Hex could stop herself. Grundzilla stared at her, uncomprehending. "Uh, never mind. You were saying?"

"I tried buying one of those Light thaums, you know, but I didn't realize until I got home that you can only activate them with magic!"

"So . . . you want a human around to activate a Light thaum so you can read your book?" Hex asked.

"Yes! I mean, there's other small tasks I'd like human magic for too, but let's start with that one."

"Um, just hypothetically, would you let me go if I told you I couldn't do magic?"

"Let you go? Of course not. I mean, it'd be a definite downer, but kidnapping you won't have been a total waste of time. *I'm* a pescatarian, but my boyfriend loves a human roast." Grundzilla paused. "You *can* do magic, right?"

Hex nodded vehemently. "Yep. Yes. Very much—yes, I can do a lot of magic. I'm fantastic at it. The best. It was just a hypothetical question."

"Right, I thought so. You came highly recommended."

"I—what?"

"I was going to kidnap another human, but she told me she was awful at Light spells and there was this other girl farther down the road who was the *real* expert." Grundzilla looked altogether too pleased with herself for having found the "real" expert.

"Who exactly recommended me?" Hex asked, although she already knew the answer.

"Oh, it was this blue-haired kid. Scrawny, missing half her eyebrows—"

"I AM GOING TO MURDER HER!" Hex bellowed.

"Well, I thought about murdering her, but I'm really trying to keep my boyfriend on a low-human diet. Humans are unhealthy and you can catch all kinds of diseases if you don't cook them right. Have you heard about the Red-Spotted Death?"

Hex was so furious, she was barely listening to the ogress. Fuse had joked that Hex should be grateful she didn't tie her up and leave her to the monsters, but she had done pretty much exactly that. Was Cam part of it too? He seemed so nice! Grundzilla was still babbling, and Hex forced herself to calm down. She could be angry at the Clanksmiths later—if she survived this.

" . . . read about it in my cooking magazine, *Bone Appétit*," the ogress was saying. "It's this awful disease you can contract if you don't cook humans properly." Hex was pretty sure there was no such disease, but she wasn't about to correct the ogress if she thought eating humans was a health hazard. Grundzilla shook her head with a look of revulsion. "Anyway, let me get this Light thaum and we can get started."

The ogress went to her bookshelf and took a thaum from one of the high shelves. She pressed the small piece of metal stamped with the word *light* into Hex's hand and then looked at her expectantly.

A Light thaum went off in Hex's head. Hadn't Cam mentioned something about using the clank in the tin box to make light? She hoped desperately the book he gave her—*The Curious Book of Clank*—explained how it worked.

"Oh, um . . . this thing?" Hex said, looking at the thaum in her hand. Her own voice sounded hesitant and fake. She really needed to sell this lie if she wanted Grundzilla to believe her. What if she pretended she was telling one of her stories? After all, lying was kind of like storytelling. Hex tried again, this time trying to sound incredulous. "Who sold you this?"

"I got it from a traveling merchant." Grundzilla's eyes narrowed in suspicion. "Why?"

"You got ripped off," Hex said. "This isn't active anymore."

"What?" Grundzilla demanded. "No—he told me the blue glow means it's still got magic left!"

Hex shrugged as much as the ropes would let her. "Maybe a bit, but not enough to make light. Look. *Light!*" Not unexpectedly, nothing happened.

"I'm going to find that merchant and cook him into a meatloaf," Grundzilla growled. Hex gulped—she was pushing her luck. "Can't you just do a Light spell without the thaum?"

"I can," Hex said, "but keeping a spell active for that long gets tiring pretty fast. And it's not that bright—but," she added quickly as the ogress clenched her fists, "I've got, ummm . . . a Light thaum in my backpack."

Grundzilla let out a long breath, and then smiled. Hex felt queasy staring at those humongous teeth. If she couldn't make this clank stuff work, she would get a much more personal tour of ogre dental hygiene. "Why didn't you just say so before?"

"It's a new type of thaum," Hex said. "It's this year's model, just released. I haven't even had the chance to study how to use it yet, but I have the newest edition of *Spellman's Dictionary* in my bag, so I'm sure I can figure it out." There was no such thing as a newer model of a thaum, but Hex hoped the ogress didn't know that.

Grundzilla mulled over this a moment. "All right," she said. "I'll untie you and let you try your thaum. Don't even *think* about running away."

Hex nodded, and Grundzilla tore through the ropes binding Hex as if they were cobwebs. She lifted Hex onto the table, then pulled Hex's backpack out of a pocket. Hex held her breath and opened *The Curious Book of Clank*, squinting in the dim light to make out the words.

An Introduction to Clank. This book will introduce you to some of the basics of clank through a number of simple projects. Rather than go into depth on any single discipline—each of which would require an entire book to simply understand the basics—this book aims to introduce new Clanksmiths to the breadth and capabilities of clank.

"Well?" Grundzilla demanded. She squinted at the book, trying to read over Hex's shoulder. The writing must have been too small for her huge ogre eyes because she huffed in frustration and gave up.

"Sorry," Hex said, toying with her NO MAJIK GURL necklace.

"New book—I just need to figure out what page the spell is on." She flipped to the table of contents and scanned through it, trying to look confident. The chapter titles might as well have been in another language: *Introduction to Physics, Basic Electronics, Batteries, Light-Emitting Diodes, Sensors, Motors, Basic Mechanics, Simple Machines, Springs and Stored Energy* . . . Her eyes traced back to *Light-Emitting Diodes*. She had no idea what a diode was but "light-emitting" sounded promising, so she turned to that page.

The first page of the chapter had a picture of a thimble-shaped device with two long prongs jutting out of it. The caption underneath read: *Light-Emitting Diode (LED)*. Hex read to herself, *Project 1: Light an LED*. She didn't have time to read the instructions with the ogress glaring down her back, but there was a picture. It looked like she was supposed to take something that looked a lot like a coin but was labeled "battery" and slip it between the two prongs of the LED.

"Enough reading," Grundzilla said. "Look, you *can* make this new type of thaum work, right? I don't have time for this—I'm a very busy ogress, I'll have you know! If you can't figure it out, we'll just call it a loss and I'll take you to my boyfriend's for dinner tomorrow."

Hex swallowed. "Take you to dinner" had no right to sound as foreboding as it did. "Yeah, let me just find the thaum." She flipped open the lid to Cam's tin box and had to bite her lip to stop the panic from showing on her face. She didn't recognize a single object inside. It was full to bursting with long metal wires, small silver cylinders, little black things smaller than her fingernail, and a few metal devices with handles like Cam had in his pockets.

"Those don't *look* like thaums," Grundzilla said, a hint of accusation in her tone.

"I told you, they're a newer type of thaum," Hex said. "Smaller, more portable . . . cheaper." To her immense relief, she found a few of the tiny thimble-shaped things in the mess of unfamiliar clank. They were smaller than she'd thought—no larger than her thumbnail. She also found a few of the batteries. They looked like silver coins, but they were blank except for a "+" on one side. Sweating, she slipped the battery in between the prongs of the LED.

Nothing happened.

Hex's heart stopped. This was it. Cam and Fuse had doomed her the moment they told Grundzilla to take her instead of them. Her death would not be in vain. She would find a way to come back as a ghost and haunt those lousy Clanksmiths and annoy them with so many bad puns they'd beg the Wyrm to use their one wish just to get her to shut up.

"Well? What's taking so long?" Hex jumped at Grundzilla's voice.

"I, uh . . ." Hex's head swum with panic. She looked at the book again, trying to figure out what she'd missed. Battery, LED . . . what else was there? Then she saw it—the prongs on the LED were two different lengths, with the plus side of the battery facing the longer prong. She flipped the battery the other way around. Instantly, the LED flared to life.

Hex dropped it in astonishment, and the light went out as the battery rolled away.

"I—I made light," she said, agog. "I . . ."

She was at an utter loss for words. After all these years of watching normal people create light with just a word and a gesture, she'd just done it herself. Without magic.

"It's not as bright or as big as I'd hoped," Grundzilla said, completely oblivious to the fact Hex was going through a major life revelation. "You don't suppose you can make it more like a lamp, so I can put it on the table as I read?"

"A lamp . . ." Hex murmured, still not processing what had just happened. She blinked twice. "Oh yeah," she said. "There's a couple more LE—um, thaums in here." An idea struck her. "Do you have a frosted glass cup or something?"

"I've got some jars," Grundzilla said, walking toward a cabinet, "but they're not frosted."

Hex rummaged through the box for something she could use to tie the batteries to the LEDs. She found a spool of black ribbon and started to unwind it, then stopped in confusion. Was it sticking to her fingers? She peeled it off her thumb and forefinger and examined it— it was like it had a Stick spell on one side. As a test, she pulled off a longer piece and stuck it to the table. It didn't come off. Forget about ever using string again, she needed a bunch of this sticky ribbon!

One by one, Hex used the ribbon to stick a battery into place between the wires of each LED. Every time an LED blinked to life, a thrill ran down Hex's spine. The day Spanner had first learned to activate a Light thaum, they'd spent hours playing with it, trying to figure out if anything besides the incantation could turn it off. They'd dropped the coin-sized thaum into one of their mom's vases of flowers to see if the water would extinguish its light. It didn't, but something else incredible happened. The frosted glass vase had lit up, the light from the single tiny thaum spreading across its entire surface. They tried again without water in the vase to see what happened. When it *still* worked, they figured out it was the translucent frosted surface, not the water, that had made the light shine so evenly.

And if that worked for a thaum, why not these LEDs?

"How about this?" Grundzilla plunked a glass jar onto the table. It looked small for the ogress, but to Hex it was the size of a bucket. It wasn't frosted, but that was okay—Hex had another idea.

"Perfect," Hex said. "One more thing—do you have a sheet of white paper?" While Grundzilla fetched one, Hex stuck the LEDs to the bottom of the jar and to the inside of the lid. The ogress returned with the paper, and Hex used it to line the inside of the jar, then screwed the lid on. This time, even Grundzilla gasped. The jar looked like they'd trapped a piece of sunlight inside. The thin white paper diffused the

light so the whole thing lit up with a pleasant glow.

"This is perfect!" Grundzilla exclaimed. "Just what I need for reading! That scrawny human knew what she was talking about when she recommended you!"

Hex allowed herself a relieved smile. "Thanks," she said. "So, will you let me go now?"

The ogress stared at Hex. "Are you kidding? No, no, you're *far* too useful. I'm going to keep you around forever!"

EGRESS FROM AN OGRESS

Grundzilla tied Hex up again while she bustled around the cave doing chores—sweeping the floor with a broom the height of a baby tree, doing laundry in a boat-sized bucket, and frying fish in a pan large enough for Hex to bathe in. *Or boil in*, Hex thought with a shudder. Fortunately, Grundzilla didn't ask Hex to perform any more magic.

It was difficult to tell how much time had passed in the dingy darkness of the cave, but Hex guessed it must be well past midnight. Grundzilla showed no sign of sleepiness, which made sense—ogres were supposed to be nocturnal.

At some point, Grundzilla untied Hex and offered her some fish to eat. Hex had to admit, the recipe from *Bone Appétit* was delicious, although she couldn't help but wonder if the original recipe called for fish or something more . . . human.

"Since you'll be living here for good, I won't tie you back up," Grundzilla said when Hex was done eating her (perfectly seasoned) fish. "And because I'm so generous, I'll even let you have your stuff back. But if you try any funny business, my boyfriend's no-human diet is off, if you know what I mean."

Grundzilla settled in next to her new lamp to read. Hex made herself a bed by folding an ogress-sized handkerchief and setting it on a kitchen chair. She had no intention of ever *using* the bed, but she wanted Grundzilla to think she was cooperating.

Before lumbering into her bedroom, Grundzilla barricaded the front door by dropping a large wooden beam onto two brackets. "And don't forget to turn off the lamp," she told Hex. Then she was gone, leaving Hex alone in the room. There was nothing to stop Hex from lifting the beam out, opening the door, and leaving. Nothing, except that the beam was several feet above her head and at least twice as long as she was tall. Even if she could do magic, she couldn't think of a single spell in *Spellman's Dictionary* that would get her out right now—the beam was far too heavy for a single person to levitate without a chunk of thaumium the size of her head.

Hex estimated she had lost the entire night stuck in the cave while the Clanksmiths and the other wish hunters raced closer to the Wyrm and *her* wish. She had to get out of here, and not only because of the wish. If she didn't escape soon, Grundzilla would realize Hex couldn't actually do magic. Now was her chance, while Grundzilla was asleep. It was just like one of her No Magic Girl stories—she just needed to come up with a clever way out. She grabbed her sketchbook and drew by the light of the lamp. If she could pull one end of the crossbeam on the door up from its bracket, she could rotate the whole thing up and out. Her eye fell on the coat rack by the door, and an idea started forming on the page.

She finished drawing and was itching to execute her plan, but she forced herself to wait. She had no idea if Grundzilla was actually asleep yet or just lying in her bed counting color-changing sheep. After what seemed like forever, Grundzilla began to snore.

Hex slung her backpack on, then slid down from the giant chair and made her way over to the coat rack. With her rope looped over her shoulder, Hex climbed to the top using Grundzilla's coats as hand- and footholds, leaving dirty footprints on a very nice cream-colored jacket. The coat rack was iron, solidly built, and had a wide, heavy-looking base, so it didn't even shake as Hex made her way up. She put her backpack in the giant breast pocket of Grundzilla's cream coat, then sat on an empty hook with her legs dangling above the beam that barricaded the door.

She tied a loop in the rope, lowered it so she could snag the end of the beam, and yanked the knot tight. Perfect. Now, she just needed to hoist up the end of the beam. She pulled up on the rope. The beam didn't budge. She pulled harder, leaning back until she was practically horizontal. When that didn't work, she hung the rope over the hook and slowly lowered herself onto it so she was dangling in midair with her entire body weight on it. Nothing.

Hex ground her teeth and climbed up the rope and back onto her perch. What was she expecting? The beam was probably the size and weight of a baby sea serpent.

What about *The Curious Book of Clank?* Reluctantly, she slid it out of her bag. It irked her that she was once again depending on the book those backstabbers had given her.

She didn't know exactly what she was looking for as she skimmed through. Words she didn't recognize like *capacitor* and *kinetic* jumped out at her, along with strange diagrams of blocks and pictures of coiled wire. There was not a single incantation or hand gesture diagram. Why couldn't there be a chapter called *How to Break Out of an Ogre's Cave* or even *How to Pick Up Really Heavy Objects?* No—there was no quick or obvious solution like there'd been with the LED. Maybe no solution at all.

As Hex flipped through the book, she realized more and more how different clank was from magic. Maybe the result looked the same in some ways, but the process of making clank was something else entirely. With magic, you just needed to look up the appropriate spell in *Spellman's Dictionary*, and the answer was already there. There was no such thing with clank it seemed.

She turned to a chapter called *Simple Machines*. Simple sounded good right now. The chapter surprised her. Some of it didn't seem like clank, it just seemed like ordinary . . . *stuff*. For instance, the bits about ramps and wheels. But then other parts were completely foreign to her, like the sections about "screws" and "gears."

She stopped at a picture of a person pulling up a large box using a rope wrapped around a number of small wheels. *By providing a mechanical advantage, pulleys can be used to lift or haul heavy loads. They can also be used to . . .*

This was exactly what she needed right now. There were different arrangements of wheels—or pulleys—with rope winding through them. One of them showed three pulleys—two hanging from the ceiling and a third hanging below from a rope looped around all three. There was also some math Hex didn't understand, using letters instead of numbers. Even if she couldn't comprehend most of it, the end result was clear. "W"—the weight of the box being hoisted up in the picture—was divided by three in this arrangement. Because of the way the rope snaked through the various pulleys, Hex would need to pull a longer length of rope, but the tradeoff was that she wouldn't have to lift the beam's full weight.

Hex sketched again, using the picture in the book to guide her design. Luckily, she managed to find a handful of pulleys in Cam's box of clank. Her years of experience climbing trees in her yard came in handy as she climbed off the coat hook and hung directly onto the central pole, using handfuls of fabric from Grundzilla's jackets for grip. She arranged the pulleys so they matched the picture in *The Curious Book of Clank*: two hanging on the coat hook and a third underneath. She tied a shorter length of rope between the hanging pulley and the beam. Then she climbed down to the ground, carrying the loose end of the rope with her. According to the book, when Hex pulled the rope down from her position at the base of the coat rack, the pulleys would redirect the force of her pull *up*. She repacked her sketchbook, *The Curious Book of Clank*, and Cam's box—if this worked, she would have to be ready to make a run for it.

Hex took a deep breath, her fists tight around the end of the rope. Then she *pulled!* She threw the entire weight of her body against the rope. The beam shifted. Hex pulled again, grunting with exertion, and the beam actually *moved*. More! She needed to lift the beam up farther.

Gritting her teeth, she dragged the rope toward her, hand over hand. Her arms quaked and her muscles burned, but the beam was *rising!* She could do this! The beam was now fully out of the first bracket and balanced precariously on the lip of the second bracket. If she could pull it just a little bit higher . . .

Hex threw her entire body backward in a gigantic heave. The beam lurched out of the far bracket and the rope ripped through her sweaty hands, yanking her back upright and almost pulling her up with it. The huge wooden beam crashed to the floor with a sound like one of the Thunder Knight's blasts of lightning, and the door creaked open the smallest sliver.

Grundzilla's snoring stopped.

8

A BAD SIGN

"Human?" Grundzilla's voice rumbled from the other room, still drowsy. "What are you doing, making such a racket?"

The ogress' heavy footsteps echoed through the cave. Hex grabbed her backpack and yanked the edge of the door, squinting against the cold rain blowing in from outside. A little wider and she could squeeze through . . .

It was like trying to move a mountain—there was no way Hex could get the door open in time. She dashed to the bookcase and crouched behind the complete collection of *The Amorous Adventures of Amalda the Alchemist*.

The floor shook as Grundzilla stepped into the room. Hex held her breath in case the ogress could hear her.

"Human?" Grundzilla said again.

There was a pause, then—

"HUUUMAN!"

A *bang* rocked the cave, and cold wind and rain blew into the room. Grundzilla must have thrown open the door, probably thinking Hex had already escaped. She roared and thundered out.

Hex waited a moment before scurrying over to the door and peeking through. She caught the briefest glimpse of Grundzilla's face contorted in rage before she dove back behind the door. Had Grundzilla spotted her?

The ogress' footsteps pounded back into the cave. Hex froze. There was nowhere she could go.

"Where's my darn raincoat?" Grundzilla muttered. Hex heard a swish of fabric, then more footsteps as the ogress left the cave again.

Relief swept through Hex and it took her a moment to remember how to breathe again. She waited a few minutes for Grundzilla's bellows to grow farther away. Then she slipped out through the door and into the early dawn. Heart thumping, she snuck through the boulders and stony debris, silently thanking the torrential rain for covering the sound of her footsteps. Once she was sure she was out of Grundzilla's line of sight, she ran. The ground was rocky and uneven, and she tripped, hitting her knee hard against stone. She scrambled back up and kept running, stumbling and sliding over rocks, until the angry yells of the ogress were far behind her.

Hex didn't know how long she'd been running when the rain stopped and the sun finally peered over the horizon. She collapsed against a rock and surveyed her surroundings. She was so tired! But she could sleep on the carriage to Midbar.

She'd been running downhill most of the way and had descended from whatever mountain peak Grundzilla lived on. She was still high up enough to see a road winding its way through the valley then branching almost directly below her. One road led through a dense forest and to a small town, the other took a longer route around the forest before reconnecting.

Hex opened her map and tried to pinpoint her exact location. Road through a valley, forest, and town . . . there! She planted her finger on the map and laughed. Grundzilla had carried Hex directly over the mountains, which the road went all the way around. If she was reading the landscape correctly, the town she was seeing was Pixbie, on the same coach route she needed but miles closer to Midbar. By sheer luck Hex had made it back to the road, already well past Blinkenburgh and where she would have gotten had she not been kidnapped. Fuse had been trying to get rid of her, but instead Hex might even be *ahead* of the Clanksmiths.

Feeling reenergized, Hex clambered down the mountain. From her view on high, she saw several other travelers farther back on the road. How many of them were also after the wish? The rising sun glinted off the top of the closest carriage, and Hex shaded her eyes to get a better view. It was difficult to see from this distance, but the distinctive glass roof made it stand out even from her perch on the mountain. It was the Clanksmiths.

Hex grinned. If she hurried, they wouldn't even see her overtaking them. She raced down the mountain, occasionally stumbling where it became steep. She stopped at the wooden signpost where the road forked. It had two arrows, one reading "Pixbie: 7 miles" and the other "Pixbie, via Puckhaven Woods: 2 miles." Hex didn't even hesitate as she headed down the shorter route—the sooner she got to Pixbie, the faster she could get a carriage to Midbar.

Another sign, not yet weathered and stained like the one at the fork, was pounded into the ground a few yards down the road. *DANGER: DO NOT ENTER FOREST. FAIRIES.*

Hex stopped and groaned. She knew the stories. Fairies were vain and a bit airheaded, but they had a vicious streak—like the sort of children who pulled off the wings of flies for fun. Their magic was also different from human magic—it was less permanent, but more powerful. They would transform humans into slugs or worms, and by the time the human changed back fifteen minutes later, they'd already be in the stomach of a hungry bird. Hex didn't want to take the longer route, but she didn't see much choice. Walking into fairy territory was asking for disaster.

She started to turn back the other way, and then stopped again. A wicked grin spread across her face.

She went back to the *DANGER* sign, yanked it out of the ground and hid it under a bush. By the time the Clanksmiths— and any other wish hunter—managed to escape the fairies, Hex would be well on her way to Midbar. She ducked behind a tree just as the Clanksmith's car rumbled into view. A moment later they disappeared into the forest. Hex was unable to suppress a smirk. Served them right.

She started down the long road around the forest, and as the adrenaline began to wear off, her smile melted. What if the Clanksmiths got seriously hurt? People foolish or careless enough to enter a forest infested with fairies didn't always make it out again.

They almost got you killed, a nasty voice inside her said.

Hex tilted her chin up and kept walking. They'd be fine, they had their crummy clank. She should just forget—

A muffled yell cut through the forest, followed by high-pitched, maniacal giggling.

Hex froze in her tracks. She wanted the Clanksmiths out of her way, not *hurt*.

But she needed that wish more than she'd ever needed anything before.

And yet, Cam had saved Hex from being trampled by a fire-breathing cow, even at the cost of falling behind on his own journey to the Wyrm.

Why should she risk her life for them?

How could she leave Cam behind?

"Curse you, conscience!" Hex shouted, and took off at a run into the forest.

She wasn't even sure how her legs still carried her. She hadn't slept a wink in Grundzilla's cave, but she pushed ahead anyway. The sun had fully risen when she'd entered the forest, but now she had to strain her eyes to see as the dense foliage pressed in on her. The sounds of twittering birds grew muffled, then died altogether. She shivered—something was *wrong* about this forest.

She didn't run far before she saw a large, familiar object by the side of the road. The Clanksmiths' car.

Hex opened her mouth to call out for them, then snapped it shut. An eerie music whispered through the oppressive silence. A fairy revel was nearby. If Hex started shouting for the Clanksmiths now, the fairies would hear her.

She crept farther down the road, ducking into the shadows of the surrounding trees as a soft golden glow filtered through the forest and the music grew louder. A large clearing up ahead revealed the revel. There must have been at least a hundred of the creatures, no larger than toddlers, all dressed in gowns and suits made of flowers, leaves, tree bark, and vines. Some of them hovered in the air, iridescent wings fluttering, while others draped themselves lazily on beds of moss and leaves.

And they all sparkled. Hex gagged. No self-respecting humanoid *sparkled*.

Where were the Clanksmiths? She didn't see them among the fairies, but they must be close. She scanned the forest just outside the clearing and her eyes landed on several enormous spheres made of thick vines hanging from the trees like gigantic fruit. Each sphere had a small window woven into the vines. And through one of those windows, Hex could just make out a head of black hair with a pair of blue goggles perched on top.

Hex gulped. How in the world could she free Cam and Fuse without the fairies noticing? Maybe she could sneak—

Something tapped Hex on the shoulder. She jumped, then turned around slowly. A glittery green face grinned back at her.

"Busted!" the fairy chirped.

9

A FAIRY TOUGH SITUATION

"Hey, nice to see you again!" Cam said, beaming as Hex was thrown into the cage. The vines, which the fairies had magically parted to make an entrance, wove back together. "How'd you get caught?"

She did not smile back. She was relieved they were still alive, but she was angry at herself for being captured, and even angrier at Fuse. Fuse stared at her with an expression she recognized all too well—it was the mulish way Spanner looked when he'd been caught stealing sweets but refused to apologize. Hex wanted to yell at them right then and there, but squished down that impulse. They needed to get out of this forest first.

"I got spotted by the fairies, same as you," Hex said, neglecting to mention why any of them were in the forest in the first place. "Got any ideas how we can—"

"Unhand me, you vile creatures!"

Hex, Cam, and Fuse all rushed to the small window to see who was shouting. The voice was deep and majestic and somehow . . .

familiar? A gaggle of fairies flew up past the small window in their cage, carrying two men in armor up to another vine sphere hanging above and to the side of theirs. Hope surged through Hex when she saw the larger man's black and gold chest plate.

"It's the Thunder Knight," Hex whispered. "We're saved!" Obviously, getting captured by fairies was a spot of bad luck, but how often did one get the chance to be rescued by the Thunder Knight himself?

Cam's eyes went round as coins. "*The* Thunder Knight?"

"I saw him on the way here," Hex said. "He's been patrolling the roads, keeping them safe for innocent travelers."

"Didn't stop him from getting captured by a bunch of fairies," Fuse snorted.

"Yeah, well, you got captured too," Hex pointed out, and Fuse scowled at her.

"I will vanquish you! I will—" The fairies threw the Thunder Knight into the cage, and his bellowing was cut off with a thud and a grunt.

The sound of tinkly, cruel laughter rose around them. "Have fun trying to vanquish us from your cage, Knighty-Poo! Twizzle Blossom, take the Thunder Knight's ginger friend. We'll start with him."

"No! Let go of Percival!" the Thunder Knight shouted in his deep baritone. "*Lightning*!" A bolt of lightning shot out of his vine cage, but the fairies dodged it easily, giggling as they dragged off the struggling attendant.

"Mr. Thunder Knight?" Hex called out.

"What? More prisoners?"

"Yeah, there's three of us in the cage under you."

The Thunder Knight's face appeared at the small window in his cage, perfectly chiseled with just the right amount of rugged scruffiness.

"You look like mere children!"

"Um. I'm twelve?" Hex said.

"Those dastardly fairies, kidnapping children! Fear not! I will save us! After all, this is nothing compared to the time I rescued the prince of Runemont from the clutches of an evil goblin horde. Can you see what has become of my dear companion Percival? I'm afraid my cage is facing the wrong way."

Hex, Cam, and Fuse turned their gaze from the Thunder Knight to the clearing just in time to see the fairies encase Percival in a translucent blue bubble.

"Um, I think they're playing catch with him," Hex said.

"Ah, is that all? That doesn't seem so horrible. Percival has an excellent throwing arm."

"Let me clarify, they're playing catch with him as the ball."

There was a brief silence.

"That sounds . . . uncomfortable," the Thunder Knight said.

"Yeah, it does look uncom—ouch, they just dropped him." Hex winced.

"We must rescue him immediately. *Open!*" He spoke the last word with the intonation of a spell, but nothing happened. "Curse it, they must have enchanted it."

"Sir? The entire thing is made of vines. Pretty sure we can just cut or burn right through it anyway," Hex said.

"Ah, you're right! *Slic—*"

"Don't finish that spell!" Fuse interrupted. "Didn't you see how high up we are? Anyway, those fairies are gonna see us dropping down from the trees and they'll just trap us again."

"Hmm . . . you speak wisely," the knight replied after a brief pause.

"If by wisely, you mean using common sense, then sure. Look, Mr. Thunderface, we gotta distract those fairies."

"And find a way to get down," the Thunder Knight added. "We're too heavy to levitate to the ground safely, unless you happen to have a whole lot of thaumium with you."

"No, but we have a rope!" Cam offered.

"Can you do a Lightning spell to distract them?" Hex asked.

"I'm afraid not. The dastardly fiends took all my thaumium, and I just used my emergency piece on that last blast," the Thunder Knight said. "Be patient just a little longer and I will draw up a bold, fearless plan to distract the fairies and then use the rope to escape my cage and rescue you! Be steady, my brave children!" His face disappeared from the window as he got to planning.

Fuse plopped down on the leafy cage floor. "All right, now that that clown's distracted, how're we getting out of here?"

"Clown?" Hex repeated. "That's the Thunder Knight! If anyone can figure it out, it's him!"

Fuse rolled her eyes. "I'd bet what's left of my eyebrows that at this very moment, he's searching the pocket edition of *Spellman's Dictionary* for the word 'Distract'."

"Is that a real spell?" Cam asked. "Sounds useful."

"No, Cam, it's not."

Hex shook her head. "You're wrong, Fuse. The Thunder Knight's gone on hundreds of adventures and saved thousands of people. I'm sure he's clever enough to figure out the right spell to make a distra—"

"Children," the Thunder Knight called out. "Would any of you happen to know any synonyms for *distract* or perhaps *confound*?"

"Try *amuse*," Fuse shouted back. She raised her eyebrows and grinned smugly at Hex.

Hex's heart sank. "Wait, that's the best he can think of?"

"Normies," Fuse scoffed. "They're too used to magic to think creatively."

Cam shrugged. He looked disappointed but unsurprised. "So, brainstorm then?"

"What's a brain . . . storm?" Hex asked, envisioning a bunch of slimy brains caught in a tornado.

"It's a way to come up with ideas by drawing them out and talking about them." Cam pulled out a handful of crumpled papers and pens from one of his many pockets. "Just like those pictures in your sketchbook."

Hex peered out the window. "They're taking turns seeing how high they can bounce Percival now. Do we have time for a brainstorm?"

"We'll be fast," Cam said. "If we just jump in without thinking about the clank first, it'll be a lot harder to make something good."

"I hadn't thought of it like that," Hex admitted as Cam and Fuse started scribbling.

"We throw explosives at them." Fuse threw down a sheet of paper with a drawing of stick figures and a big squiggly mess.

"We could build a gun that stuns them." Cam tossed his drawing next to Fuse's. His sketch was hardly any better than hers, but Hex began to understand. The point wasn't to create a fully formed idea or a beautiful drawing—it was to quickly generate ideas and share them.

"We could build some kind of a moving machine to distract them," Fuse suggested.

"What's a machine?" Hex studied Fuse's picture for an answer, but it was incomprehensible. Drawing didn't seem to be her strongest suit.

"Um . . ." Cam drummed his fingers on his knee. "It's a thing you build out of clank that you put energy into to make it move or do something."

"I'll be done formulating a plan soon, children!" the Thunder Knight assured them.

"I'm sure you will!" Fuse sang back.

Cam glanced up at Hex. "You haven't drawn anything yet."

Hex put her pencil to the paper, feeling foolish. "I don't even know how clank works or what materials we have to work with . . ."

"Don't overthink it. Just draw anything that pops into your head," Cam said. "You've got ideas, and we've got the clank know-how."

What if this was just another one of her stories? No Magic Girl versus the fairies . . .

"Maybe we could attach some kind of decoy to a tiny version of Cam's go-cart motor thing?" Hex hesitantly added her first drawing to the rest. But the Clanksmiths nodded in acknowledgement of her idea. "Or . . . is there a way to make a loud noise on the other side of the clearing?" This was just a story, and Hex knew stories. The ideas flowed from her brain, through her pencil, and onto the paper. "Can we use one of Fuse's sparkly fire things? How about a slingshot to shoot something at them? Or could we build a flying thing that drops stuff on them? Is that possible with clank? What if we use LEDs to blind them—are they bright enough?"

"Wow, Hex!" Cam exclaimed. Hex looked up and found the other two staring at her.

"Am I brainstorming wrong?" Hex asked, suddenly self-conscious.

"No!" Cam said. Even Fuse's patchy eyebrows were raised in grudging admiration. "This is great! Look, we can combine some of these ideas." He moved some of the sheets together. "I like the idea of using one of Fuse's chemical concoctions as a distraction—"

"Smoke bombs!" Fuse said. "I've got a handful in my pocket."

"And if we can shoot a few down to the clearing with the slingshot, the fairies won't see us leaving the cage!" Cam continued.

"I don't know what a smoke bomb is, but it sounds like a distraction!" Hex said. "Then the Thunder Knight can cut through his cage, summon the rope, and get us out of here!"

"Or," Fuse said, "we cut through our *own* cage and leave that blowhard behind!" Hex and Cam glared at Fuse. She grinned and shrugged. "Well, if he's as great as he thinks he is, he should be fine without us." She produced a handful of caramels, each with a thick green string sticking out from the middle.

"Candy?" Hex asked.

"Don't eat those," Fuse said. "They're smoke bombs—potassium nitrate, sugar, and visco fuse." Why were the Clanksmiths always speaking in their own strange language? Fuse peered out the window of the cage and frowned. "I don't think the slingshot is gonna work. There's too many tree branches in the way. The smoke bombs might just get caught in the leaves and go off right next to us. Got any other ideas?"

"Ugh, I guess that plan just went up in *smoke*." Hex grinned.

"Does that even count as a pun?" Cam asked. "Hex, I think you kinda *bombed* that joke."

"Stop it, both of you," Fuse groaned. Cam gave Hex a high five before turning back to sift through the pile of papers.

"Hex, what's this?" he asked, pointing to one of Hex's brainstorming sketches.

"Oh, it's supposed to be a small version of your go-cart," Hex said. "I thought you could use it as a distraction, but I don't really know how . . ." She trailed off and looked out the window. Fuse was right, there were a number of tree branches in the way. But if she pressed her face to the window and stood on her tiptoes, she could just make out the forest floor and a clear path directly to where the fairies were. "What if we put the smoke bomb on a tiny go-cart, lower it, and drive it to where the fairies are? Is that possible?"

"Ohhhh!" Cam said. "Hex, that's brilliant!"

"Do we even have enough clank to build it?" Hex asked, suddenly skeptical of her own suggestion.

"I've got enough stuff in my pockets to make a simple motorized cart we can put the smoke bombs on. We won't be able to control it, but if we can get it pointed in the right direction, it'll just go on its own!"

"And then we can get it close enough so the bombs go off right in the middle of their party!" Fuse finished. "Nice job, Hex!" She punched her on the shoulder in a friendly way, then grimaced. "Forget I did that, I temporarily forgot we're rivals."

"Mr. Thunder Knight!" Hex shouted to the other cage. "We've got a plan to make a distraction!"

"Excellent! Obviously, I had a plan as well—several, actually—but I deemed them to be too dangerous for children."

"Obviously," Fuse muttered, rolling her eyes. "How's our buddy Percival doing?"

"They're still bouncing him. He looks like he's about to throw up," Cam said.

Hex didn't help so much as watch with fascination as the ideas she'd scrawled out on paper became a reality. She didn't know clank well enough for any of her ideas to be more than concepts, but that was all Cam and Fuse needed to cobble together bits and pieces of wire, wood, and clank to make something that, until now, had never before existed. And that act of creation was somehow even more impressive than any magical spell.

The result looked like one of Spanner's toys, but with a battery and a little metal cylinder Cam said was like a tiny version of the motor on his go-cart. Fuse finished it off by tying the smoke bombs to the top of the cart with wire.

"All right, let's do this." Fuse drew out a small metal rectangle and flicked it with a finger. It ignited a tiny flame.

"What—what is that?" Hex gaped at it.

"It's a lighter," Cam said. "It's kind of like a Fire spell."

"I am *never* using flint again."

"Actually, it's got a piece of flint—" Cam started.

"Shh, don't ruin my moment," Hex said.

Fuse pulled on her goggles. "Safety glasses. Gotta wear 'em when you light smoke bombs," she advised Hex, handing her a pair from one of her many pockets.

"Or you'll burn off half your eyebrows like Fuse," Cam said, lowering his own goggles over his eyes. Well, that explained Fuse's patchy eyebrows.

"Eyebrows schmeyebrows, it's your eye*balls* you gotta worry about. Safety third—"

"Safety *first*, Fuse," Cam corrected.

"That's what I said."

"Mr. Thunder Knight," Hex called out. "Get ready!"

Fuse lit the green strings and Cam pushed a button on the cart. The wheels spun on with a high-pitched whirring. Fuse and Hex lifted Cam up so he could stick his head out the window to get a better view of the forest floor below. He lowered the cart slowly

using a length of twine.

"Almost there," he muttered. "Come on . . . it's spinning, I just need to wait until it faces the right way. Aaand . . . it's on the ground!" he announced, letting go of the twine.

"Bing . . ." Fuse said.

"There it goes!" Cam exclaimed, and Hex stood on her toes to watch the small cart trundle toward the gathering of fairies.

"Bang . . ." Fuse said.

"Mr. Thunder Knight—get ready with that Slice spell!" Hex shouted.

"Boom!" Fuse yelled.

Plumes of gray-white smoke poured into the air, making it look like a cloud had fallen from the sky and crashed into the clearing. Fairies fluttered through the air like a flock of startled firebirds, squawking in alarm.

"*Slice*!" the Thunder Knight intoned, ripping a gash through the side of his cage. He parted the vines like a curtain and poked his head out. "Excellent, children! The rope!"

Cam thrust it through the window of their cage, and the Thunder Knight used a spell to summon it up and into his waiting hands. Some of the fairies stumbled out of the smoke, coughing. The Thunder Knight tied the rope to his cage, then slid down it until he was level with Hex, Cam, and Fuse.

His face went tight with concern when he saw them clustered

in the window. "You're so young! What in the world led you poor children here?"

"We're looking for the Wi—"

Fuse clapped a hand over Cam's mouth. "—the way out!" she rushed to finished. "We're looking for the way out of the forest."

The Thunder Knight's brow creased. "You're . . . looking for . . ." He paused.

"Um, Mr. Thunder Knight," Hex said. "Not to worry you or anything, but the smoke's starting to fade. We need to move."

He ignored Hex and fixed his gaze on Cam. "You're looking for the Wishing Wyrm. That's what you were about to say, wasn't it?"

Cam's mouth was still covered by Fuse's hand, but his eyes went wide.

"Alas, it seems the fairies have already spotted us! I'll have to come back for you with reinforcements." The Thunder Knight leaned closer to the cage, lowering his voice to a menacing growl. "*After* I've found the Wyrm."

10

A RIBBIT-ING ESCAPE

"Did the Thunder Knight just—just—" Hex opened and closed her mouth, words failing her.

"Um, Hex?"

"I can't believe I used to write stories about that good-for-nothing, pompous, phony jerk!" She was going to throw away her "I've been Thunderstruck! (Member of the Official Thunderhead Fan Club)" pin as soon as she got the chance.

"Hex, uh, the *fairies*." The fear in Cam's voice cut through the red fog of rage clouding Hex's vision, just in time for her to see a swarm of fairies surround their cage.

"Oh nooo!" one of them wailed. "Why would the Thunder Knight leave before he's had time to play with us?"

"Stop crying, Briar Berry, we still have these other humans to play with us. You'll play with us, right?"

"No," Fuse replied.

"Play with us! Play with us!" The other fairies joined in, reaching grasping hands into the cage.

"I know!" said a silver-haired fairy with a confident smile. "Let's play hide-and-seek!"

"That doesn't sound so bad," Cam said.

"And anytime we find one of you, we get to turn you into a froggy!"

"*That* does," Hex groaned.

The door flew open and tiny hands grabbed them and carried them to the forest floor. The Thunder Knight's attendant, Percival, was slumped on a pile of leaves, breathing heavily and muttering healing incantations. His red hair was ruffled, and he sported several bruises on his face.

"You okay?" Hex whispered to him. He nodded at her with a tired smile and continued enchanting his cuts and bruises away.

"I might have some bandages in my pocket—" Cam started.

"You have two minutes to hide!" interrupted the silver-haired fairy, and she and all the other fairies closed their eyes. "Starting . . . NOW!"

Hex and the Clanksmiths burst into a run, and Percival leapt up and joined them. "Where's the Thunder Knight?" he panted.

"He betrayed us," Hex spat.

Fuse—the only one not short of breath—grinned. "I would've done the same thing."

"You *did* do the same thing!" Hex retorted. She'd told herself she wouldn't bring this up until they were all safe, but Fuse's smug smile made her words explode out. "The Thunder Knight isn't the only backstabber around here! You almost got me killed!"

"I wasn't trying to get you killed, just stall you," Fuse grumbled. "There's only one wish, and it's every man—or girl or whatever— for themselves."

"Wait—*killed*? What are you talking about?" Cam demanded.

"Fuse—" Hex started.

"Shh, they'll hear which direction we're going," Percival hissed.

"You have one minute before we come find yoooou!" squealed a fairy from somewhere deep in the forest.

Hex skidded to a halt at a large tree, its lower branches within arm's reach. "What if we hide in the branches?"

"They can fly," Fuse whispered. "They'll spot us."

"There!" Cam said. "A hollow tree!" They followed him, squeezing into the small cavity.

The sound of whirring wings and tinkly laughter floated to them from the clearing. "Time's up, humans! Hide and seeeeek!"

"What did you mean Fuse backstabbed you?" Cam whispered.

"Fuse sold me out to an ogress who tried to eat me!" Hex replied, her voice barely louder than the rustling leaves outside.

Cam's eyes grew round with horror. "An ogress tried to *eat* you?"

Despite her anger and fear, a small bubble of relief floated through Hex's stomach. Cam really hadn't been a part of Fuse's ploy.

"Yes! Well, no, Grundzilla's a pescatarian. But her boyfriend's not!"

"Oh, please. Don't tell me you wouldn't do anything to get to that wish first," Fuse sneered. Hex's guilt must have shown on her face because Fuse raised an eyebrow. "Oh? Something you want to tell us?"

Hex hesitated. She didn't feel like she owed Fuse anything, but Cam was searching her face with his earnest eyes. "It's . . . it's my fault we're all stuck in here," she said finally, letting out a long, slow breath. "There was a 'DANGER: FAIRIES' sign and . . . I . . ." She swallowed the lump of shame that suddenly overwhelmed her. Her snap decision had seemed so clever in the moment, but now she felt horrible. What if they all died in this forest because of her? " . . . I figured I could get ahead, so I hid the sign. Let's call it even?"

A devious smirk flickered across Fuse's face. "What'd I tell you, Cam? She's not your friend."

"Did you really, Hex?" Cam said, looking hurt.

"Can this wait until we get out of here?" Hex asked.

"You started it," Fuse said with a shrug.

"Oooh, Pimpernel, I think I hear something!" a high voice trilled nearby. As one, Hex, Cam, Fuse, and Percival covered their mouths. The beating of wings drew closer.

A fairy with wild green hair and a triumphant smile bounced into their alcove. "Found—"

Fuse grabbed the fairy, covering its mouth with one hand, and at the same moment, Percival hissed "*Sleep*!" The fairy fell limp in Fuse's arms.

"Fern Frond?" called the first voice. "Where did you go?" The buzzing of its wings retreated, and Hex let out a breath.

"We need a plan," she whispered. "Another distraction. Something they'll chase instead of us."

"If we can get to the car, we can outrun them," Fuse said.

"What's a car?" Percival asked, looking from Fuse to Hex.

"It's . . . our nickname for our carriage," Fuse said. "Obviously."

"What about your—" Hex hesitated. "Uh, your Sparkler thaums? The ones you, uh, got from that very faraway country with foreign magic? We could set those off, then make a run for your car."

"We are all about the flammable distractions today, aren't we?" Fuse said with an impish grin. "I like it!"

Hex poked her head outside the alcove. The coast was clear. The four of them spilled out of the tree trunk, and Fuse immediately got to work, jamming the sparklers into the ground in a small bundle.

"Those are thaums?" Percival asked.

"Yep. Foreign, like Hex said. Watch." Fuse waved her hands over the sparklers in a complicated gesture, the lighter partially concealed in her palm, and in an especially dramatic voice she intoned, "*Sparkle*!"

Percival gaped as the sparklers poured out a cascade of light. Hex grabbed his wrist and pulled him, running into the cover of the trees. Fuse led the way, darting between trees like a shadow, and Hex marveled at her innate sense of direction.

"Over there!" a fairy shouted. "Where the sparkly lights are!"

Hex glanced back and saw the fairies descend on the spot where they'd planted the sparklers. She muttered a curse and sprinted even faster until she was practically shoulder to shoulder with Fuse. Cam and Percival got the message and they sped up, huffing from the exertion.

"I see them!" a fairy screamed. Hex looked over her shoulder again and wished she hadn't. The fairies flew after them in a glittering, candy-colored storm.

"There's the car—" Cam shouted, just as a fairy lassoed him around the torso with a vine.

Fuse yanked the end of the vine out of the fairy's grasp and leapt into the car, pulling Cam behind her. The car roared to life and lurched forward—away from Hex and Percival.

Hex almost forgot to keep running as shock and anger swept through her. They were going to leave her behind!

"DON'T YOU DARE, FUSE!" Cam hollered. And then the car crashed *back* through the trees, Cam at the wheel, his kind face twisted in fury. Hex ran toward them, hauling the Thunder Knight's poor attendant behind her.

"You're cheating!" a fairy squealed, grabbing Hex by the collar and dragging her back. Fuse leaned out of her seat and pulled Hex out of the fairy's grasp and into the car, although she looked none too happy about it.

"You're no fun!" another fairy screamed. Percival cast spells left and right, causing fairies to drop from the air or spin in helpless circles.

"Something's wrong with the carriage!" he shouted. "It's making all kinds of weird noises!"

"The Spin thaums are acting up, they just need to be replaced," Fuse said so smoothly that Hex was sure she used the same line every time someone asked about the car's strange roar.

Cam drove too fast for the fairies to keep up. The car smashed through the shrubs at the edge of the forest and into the sunlight, then onto the road. The fairies followed through, but more hesitantly, looking reluctant to leave their forest sanctuary. Finally, with the car pulling so far ahead, they glided back into the forest, their heads drooping in disappointment.

Cam drove all the way back to the fork in the road before pulling over. They all stumbled out, and Cam turned to Fuse. His expression would have forced even Grundzilla into submission. "Is it true what Hex said about the ogress?"

Fuse shrugged, and Hex could tell she was trying really hard to look nonchalant. But she kept clenching and unclenching her fists. "Yeah, I *guess* so. The ogress stopped the car while you were asleep, said she wanted a human to do her magical errands or whatever. I told her to take Hex instead. Figured it was an easy way to get rid of a rival. Didn't know she was gonna try to eat Hex." Cam opened his mouth to speak, but Fuse cut him off. "Before you get mad at me, did you miss how it's Hex's fault we got stuck in this fairy fiasco?"

"I came back for you!" Hex said. "And then you tried to leave me and Percival—"

"Shut up *all of you*!" Cam shouted. Hex froze, her mouth still hanging open. "Why are you both so horrible to each other? No one is getting that wish if we all get each other killed!"

"Why are we—why—" Fuse made an incoherent, frustrated noise. "Cam, did you miss the part where there's only *one* wish? It's a competition! We aren't friends, we're enemies!"

"And do you want the Thunder Knight to get that wish?" Cam said.

Fuse opened her mouth, then shut it.

"You really, really don't," Percival grumbled. They all turned to him. Hex had completely forgotten he was there. "When I first started working for him I thought, *Wow, I'll be working for one of the bravest, most famous knights in history! This'll be awesome!* That was before I found out half my job was doing all his dirty work—washing his underwear, fetching him coffee, fighting off monsters who weren't doing anything wrong—and the second half was editing his stories about his exploits. And now that I've *been* on those exploits, I can tell you, wow, does he take some creative freedom with those stories. Like, you know that really popular one about the time he fought off an army of trolls?"

"Oh, that one's great!" Hex chimed in, then remembered what the Thunder Knight had just done to them. It was hard to separate the ruthless man who'd betrayed them from the golden hero she'd grown up admiring.

"Yeah, well, did you know there were actually only two trolls? And one of them was still in trollementary school!"

Percival stopped, red in the face.

"Oh, that's—"

"I'm not done! I just needed to stop for breath! He didn't even *do* anything! *I* risked my neck, then he came in, did his little lightning thing," Percival waggled his fingers in a mockery of the Thunder Knight's signature spell, "and then took all the credit for himself! And here's the worst of it—even though he lies about half the stuff he does, he doesn't even *realize* he's not the greatest thing the world has ever known!"

"So . . . why didn't you just quit?" Hex asked.

"I kept thinking I should, but I was so worried about how it would look on my résumé, what my mom would think . . . you know how it is. I guess this was just the excuse I needed."

"What's his wish anyway?" Fuse asked.

"Immortality." Percival made a noise of disgust. "If he gets his wish, the universe will be stuck with him for *eternity*."

"Well, that's not so bad if he's saving people, right?" Cam said.

"Did you miss the part where he literally left a group of kids to be tortured by fairies?" Fuse snorted.

"Oh. Yeah."

"He only saves people for his own benefit," Percival added. "For every person he's saved, there's another two he walked over to get there. He just wants the glory. Well, glory and the royalties from the Official Thunderhead Fan Club merchandise."

Hex gritted her teeth. She *needed* that wish, more than some puffed-up knight who wanted to live forever, more than whatever it was Cam or Fuse wanted. But she was kidding herself if she thought she could get to it alone. She didn't trust Fuse one tiny bit, but if Cam could keep her in line . . . "The enemy of my enemy—"

"Is still my enemy," Fuse finished, daring Hex to argue.

"We work well as a team," Cam said, his jaw set stubbornly.

"I agree," Hex nodded. "But what do we do when we get to the Wyrm?"

"There is no *we*," Fuse said. "Cam, she can't come with us—"

Cam whipped around to face Fuse. "This is *my* wish. That means it's *my* choice." Hex blinked—she hadn't realized the wish was Cam's. "Did you forget how much clank changed your life? How much of a difference it makes to people like us?"

Fuse froze. Then she lowered her eyes and released a loud, exaggerated sigh. "Fine. A truce. We work together until we get the Thunder Knight out of the way. After that, we separate. Become rivals again. Whoever gets there first gets the wish, fair and square."

Cam pressed his lips together and his brow furrowed. Hex nodded. "Deal," she said, shaking Fuse's hand.

"All right," Cam said, and his anger disappeared as quickly as it had come. "I'm glad you're coming with us." Cam was kind and innocent, naive even, and Hex suspected people underestimated him all the time because of that. But that didn't mean he was a pushover.

Percival raised a timid hand. "Uh. Sorry to interfere in what's clearly a private conversation, but what's clank?"

"He meant to say bank. I'm learning accounting," Fuse said. "So anyway, Percy buddy, wanna be a pal and tell us what the Thunder Knight's plan is?"

Percival unfolded a map and spread it out on the ground. "There's three routes to the Great Barren from here. The Thunder Knight—and most of the other wish hunters—will take the mountain pass. I can promise you it's going to be all-out war there. I suggest you take this route." His finger traced a long line on the map that wove around and through a valley. "It'll take an extra day but you'll make up for that time by avoiding all the fighting."

"And what about the third route?" Hex pointed to another path through the mountains. "It looks like the shortest."

"It is, but it's no good. It's infested with goblins now." Percival shook his head. "Even the Thunder Knight isn't dense or reckless enough to go that way. No point in wishing to be immortal if you get killed first, right?"

"We're going that way," Fuse announced.

"Did you miss the part where I said *don't go that way?*" Percival asked.

"You didn't actually say those exact words, but yeah, I heard you," Fuse said. "Cam, what do you think?"

"Hang on—you *are* dropping me off in Pixbie first, right?" Percival looked alarmed. "No way I'm going to the Great Barren now that I'm not getting paid for it!"

"Yeah, yeah," Fuse said. "Cam?"

Cam shrugged. "Maybe the goblins aren't all that bad? And if they are, we can outrun them. Our car is really fast. Hex?"

"You don't have to join us. It's gonna be *reeeeeally* dangerous," Fuse said, a little too hopefully.

And let the Clanksmiths—or worse, the Thunder Knight—beat her to the Wishing Wyrm? Hex cracked her knuckles. "Let's do it."

IF AT FIRST YOU DON'T SUCCEED, FAIL, FAIL, AND FAIL AGAIN

"If clank is so secret, where did you learn about it anyway?" Hex asked as the car trundled along. In the half hour since they'd reset the sign and dropped Percival off in Pixbie, Hex had recounted how she escaped Grundzilla's clutches using (to Cam's delight) *The Curious Book of Clank*. They still had a few hours before they reached goblin territory, but they hadn't seen a single other wish hunter since the road forked toward the mountains.

While Fuse drove, Cam dug through the large metal trunk in the back of the car, pulling out bits and pieces of clank. A lot of it was much larger than the clank Hex had seen so far—wooden beams assembled into triangular frames, tools like a long-toothed blade, and a whirring handheld thing Cam called a "drill" that he put his goggles on to use. Hex suspected if Cam could have fit all of it into the many pockets on his lime green vest, he would have.

"We learned about clank in Clank City," Cam said.

"That's not a real place!"

"It is!" Cam protested.

"So how come I've never heard of it?"

"Same reason you never heard of clank. It's hidden far away. It's safer like that." Cam frowned. "But it means a lot of Undeveloped people wind up not knowing about clank and how much it could help them. I mean, Fuse and I became Clanksmiths by sheer luck."

"You mean, you weren't born in Clank City?" Hex asked. Cam and Fuse were so odd, it was hard to imagine them coming from ordinary backgrounds.

"Nope," Cam said. "I was nine the first time I went there."

"And in Clank City, there's lots of stuff like . . . like this?" Hex waved vaguely at the large wooden contraption Cam was busily constructing in the back of the car. He and Fuse had surprised Hex by collapsing the car's canopy, the glass panels folding neatly against each other, so there was more room to build. A normal carriage either had a fixed roof or was equipped with a Shield thaum for the rain. "What're you building anyway?"

"It's a portable trebuchet I designed!" Cam said with a proud flourish. "So we have a weapon in case we get attacked by goblins."

"I thought you said the car could outrun them!"

"Well, it never hurts to be prepared!"

"That's . . . not very reassuring." She thumped a hand on the trebuchet's solid wooden frame. "So how does it work?"

"None of your business," Fuse cut in. "Cam, stop teaching clank to our rival."

"She's on our team now!" Cam said, and Fuse rolled her eyes but didn't reply. "It uses a counterweight to launch a projectile. When I drop this weight here," he indicated a large rock he'd tied to one end, "it falls and makes the other end swing up." His left knee bounced up and down with barely contained energy.

"Why are you willing to teach me about clank?" Hex asked.

Cam gaped at Hex, looking utterly baffled. "Because . . . because clank is awesome. And you're a natural. You don't want to learn it?"

"I do," Hex said, flustered. "But, I mean . . . Fuse is right. We're rivals!"

"Exactly," Fuse grumbled.

"For the wish, sure. But when it comes to being Undeveloped, we're on the same side," Cam said. "And I thought maybe clank could help you . . ." His brows knit in concern. "It helped me."

Hex didn't know how to reply to that. It made sense—she had a problem, and he thought he could help, so he did. But what sort of person was that unconditionally generous to someone they'd just met? She twisted the beads on her necklace, uncomfortable with the burden of Cam's kindness. She didn't want to owe him anything—not if she was going to take his wish.

"Um, do you have any other questions about clank?" Cam asked. He drummed his fingers on his knees nervously, and Hex knew he was just trying to change the subject.

Can you teach me something that will help me beat you to the wish? she thought. Instead, she asked, "Why is the canopy of the car made of glass?"

Cam broke into a relieved smile. "Oh, it's not just glass. Take a look!"

He jumped up in his seat and pulled enough of the thick fabric canopy open for Hex to look inside. Each folded section had a large glass panel attached to it. Up close, white lines divided the blue-black glass into a grid pattern.

"They're solar panels!" Cam said, dropping the canopy back into place. "They convert the energy from sunlight to electricity, which we use to charge the batteries in some of our clank! Batteries are kind of like thaumium, but with electricity instead of magic."

"And these batteries power your car?"

"Ah, no. That'd be neat, but it needs too much energy. We've got some cars that use electricity in Clank City but we'd need a place to charge them on the way. This car uses a fuel called gasoline. We built an extra tank so we've got enough fuel for the journey, and we use the solar panels for anything that uses electricity."

"So . . . *The Curious Book of Clank* can teach me about all this? Like, what gasoline is, or how to convert sunlight to this electricity stuff?"

"Yes, exactly! What do you think?" Cam's eyes glittered with excitement. "Better than magic, right?"

Hex pursed her lips. It seemed an awful lot more complicated than magic. "I suppose it could be," she said finally. "Doesn't really help unless you live in Clank City."

Fuse looked briefly over her shoulder at them before turning her attention back to the road. "Your wish is to be Developed, isn't it?"

Her tone sounded accusatory, and Hex felt her face grow warm. "So what if it is?"

"What a stupid wish," Fuse said with a scowl.

"What, and that isn't Cam's wish also?"

Fuse snorted. "Why would he need magic? We got clank."

"Fine, so you Clanksmiths are too good for magic," Hex said, holding the back of Fuse's seat in a tight, angry grip. "But I'm *not* a Clanksmith, and that's not how it works where I come from."

"Well, maybe where you come from is also stupid."

"That's not fair!" Hex balled her fists. "If my wish is so stupid, what's Cam's wish then?"

"He doesn't have to tell you that—"

"Can you guys please stop fighting?" Cam begged.

"Fine," Hex snapped, slamming *The Curious Book of Clank* open. Of course Fuse would tell Hex her wish was stupid; she didn't want her to get the wish in the first place. But she had no right to presume anything about her life and—

"Hey, Hex?" Cam prodded her shoulder nervously. "I think the book'll be easier to read if it's not upside down."

Hex stared blankly at the page. A small laugh burst out of her despite herself, and she relaxed a little. "Thanks, Cam."

Hex read for the next few hours while Fuse drove in sullen silence and Cam tinkered with his trebuchet and then his broken go-cart. She barely understood the book and had to go back and reread parts more than once. One of the first chapters spent a lot of time talking about math, and forces, and things like *acceleration* and *mass*. She couldn't understand how it related to any of what the Clanksmiths had shown her.

"Can you explain to me how you go from this," she pointed to the page where incantations (the book called them "equations") like $F = ma$ were written, "to that?" She gestured at the go-cart Cam was fiddling with. "I mean, I already made some clank work. Do I really need to do all this math first?"

Cam looked up from his work. "Well . . . it helps to understand the physics to guide your design. For some projects you need more complicated math to figure out something before you build it, and other times it's faster to just try making it. A lot of clank is about building and testing, trying to understand why something failed, then redesigning it again. Even if you do all the math, your design still might not work the first time, and you usually learn a lot just from making and testing it! Fail early and fail often!"

"You want your design to *fail?*"

"Well, hopefully not the final version—but it's better to figure out fast if your initial design won't work so you can try to improve it. Pretty much nothing I build works the first time."

"Or the second, or the third, or the fourth . . ." Fuse said, just under her breath. It was the first time she'd spoken since the argument, and Hex wasn't sure if that meant she'd cooled off.

Hex bit her lip. "You know, Spanner and I used to make stuff like what I showed you in my sketchbook. It pretty much always failed, and I thought it was just because . . ."

Morgaine's harsh words came back to her, an abrasive melody she couldn't get out of her head. *Even your pathetic Mooch tricks don't work.*

Cam seemed to read Hex's mind. "Hex, failing is part of the process. It's how you learn. Knowing the physics helps because you can understand *why* it fails and make it better the next time. It's okay to fail."

"It's okay to fail . . ." Hex echoed. She'd never thought about it that way before. "You remind me of my brother Spanner. He always wants to try again and again even if something doesn't work." It was usually her who wanted to abandon a project, too ashamed of her failures.

"What's Spanner like?" Cam's eyes lit up with interest.

She touched the necklace he'd made her. "He's six years old, and he's the most adorable thing in the world," Hex said. Talking about Spanner made her heart ache unexpectedly. "And also sometimes the most annoying thing too."

Cam laughed. "My little brother's like that too. I think it's in the job description."

"How old is your brother?"

"Ten," Cam said.

Hex nodded absently, but her mind was already elsewhere, thinking about how much she missed Spanner and her family. She couldn't let them down—couldn't let her budding friendship with Cam get in her way. Her throat tightened with dread. What would happen when they defeated the Thunder Knight and became rivals again . . . and what would she have to do to get that wish?

12

GOBS OF GOBLINS

It was late at night by the time the car started climbing into the mountain pass. Sharp, craggy silhouettes closed in around them, far taller and more formidable than the smooth grassy slopes Hex had grown up with around Abrashire.

"All right, let's go over the plan if we get attacked," Cam said.

"We have a plan?" Fuse asked with a snort.

"Well, we have a lot of clank. That's almost like a plan!" Cam said. "Plan A—drive really fast. Plan B—try to talk to them nicely."

"Seriously, Cam?" Fuse demanded.

"Well, they might just be misunderstood and I don't want to hurt anyone by accident!"

"You're ridiculous."

"Plan C—I'll use the trebuchet. Fuse, you'll do your chemistry stuff, and Hex, you get the most fun job of all!" He handed her a small black device with buttons and levers.

"Seems a bit small." Hex flipped it over in her hands. "What does it do?"

"You remember my go-cart? Well, I fixed the damage from the crash *and* modified it! So now you can control it with that remote controller."

"Sorry, what do you mean *control?*" Hex recalled Belladonna at the grocer's, sliding the bread off the high shelf without ever touching it. "Like, I can stay in the car, and by using this," she held up the remote controller, "I can drive the go-cart, even though I'm not sitting in it?"

"Yep!" Cam said cheerfully. "You just use that knobbly bit to steer, and then you can drive it around to make the goblins trip and stuff!"

Hex studied the remote controller. Controlling the go-cart sounded like a lot of fun, but she wasn't so sure about this "plan." The Clanksmiths were excellent at clank . . . but so far planning wasn't their strong suit.

She had just begun thinking of other ideas when the car's headlights illuminated a fallen tree blocking the road. Fuse stopped the car and frowned. "Coincidence or trap?"

Hex and Cam didn't get a chance to reply. The night burst to life with a hundred voices howling, jeering, and screaming. All around them, goblins emerged from the darkness. They were a motley assortment—the smallest of them was no taller than Spanner and the largest were hulking beasts the size of porcubears—wearing everything from loincloths to full suits of armor.

The goblins at the front sniffed the air like they were searching for something. Then a particularly large one cracked open a wide, monstrous grin. "These humans can't do magic," it shouted to its comrades.

There wasn't even time to turn on the remote controlled go-cart before they were completely overrun. Cam released the trebuchet arm, flinging a boulder into the air. The goblins scattered but because there were so many of them, more just rushed in to fill their places, their bulbous eyes flashing in vicious yellows and reds.

"*Don't worry, we can outrun them,*" Hex grumbled. She punched one of the goblins with the remote control as it leapt into the car, its bestial face twisted in a snarl.

A pair of rough hands grabbed Hex. She tried to grab her backpack from the back seat, but the goblin pulled her away and slung her over its shoulder. Her nostrils filled with the smell of earth and sweat.

"Cam!" she yelled, but if Cam heard her, he was unable to do anything. To her left, a goblin threw Fuse over its shoulder.

Hex twisted in the goblin's grip but it was like iron. She could do nothing as her captor followed the stream of goblins into a gaping black hole in the mountainside. Hex only caught glimpses of their lair as she bounced up and down, her head bumping painfully against the goblin's metal armor. She felt a flutter of panic every time she lost sight of Cam or Fuse. With *The Curious Book of Clank* and all her supplies and building materials still in her backpack in the car, she would be helpless if she got separated from them.

The goblins carried her and the others through a long stone corridor with wooden doors, openings to cavernous rooms, and small dark tunnels. Goblins branched off from the main horde into the smaller passages, and the crowd gradually thinned.

"Ugh, humans?" a small goblin in head-to-toe green armor said, prodding Hex with the butt of a spear. "You couldn't have found something that actually *tastes* good?"

"I love a good human roast!" said a goblin in a purple dress.

The first goblin snorted. "You've clearly never tasted a proper *coq au vin* or *fairy mignon*."

"Stop being a snob, Bert."

"Yeah," the goblin carrying Hex chimed in. "Have you even *tasted* human, or are you just judging us because it's not in one of your snooty cooking magazines? Look, why don't you try a bite now while it's fresh—"

Before Hex knew what was happening, her captor flipped her over and thrust her face at Bert the goblin. Hex screamed and wriggled desperately. She couldn't see Cam or Fuse but could hear both of them shouting to let her go.

"Just try an ear," the goblin in purple added, twisting Hex's head toward Bert.

"Don't!" Hex shrieked. "I taste awful!"

Bert's entire face was hidden by a helmet except for his terrifying bright yellow eyes. They flickered right, then left, studying her like a predator considering its prey. She couldn't move, couldn't think—

"Fine, I'll try a bite at dinner," Bert said. "After it's cooked and marinated—they carry all kinds of diseases if you eat them raw."

Hex almost fainted with relief as her captor shrugged.

"Suit yourself, Bert," said the goblin in purple, exchanging a sly smile with another goblin that clearly said they were used to Bert's eccentricities.

The goblins continued down the corridor with Hex and the others. When only a small handful of goblins were left, they came to a halt in front of a barred cell and threw Hex in. Cam and Fuse followed a moment later, and the prison door slammed shut behind them.

Fuse hurled herself at the bars. "Hey!" she yelled. "Let us out!"

A small, spindly goblin cackled, "Why would we do that? Chef wants to try a new recipe tonight!"

"Yeah, well, I got a good recipe for a knuckle sandwich," Fuse shouted.

Hex grabbed her arm and pulled her back. "Don't waste time trying to argue with them," she whispered. "We need to figure out how to get out of here."

The group of remaining goblins were discussing something among themselves, gesturing at Hex, Cam, and Fuse. Words like *succulent* and *juicy* rose above the chatter and sent a nervous shiver down Hex's spine.

"How're we even going to figure a way out of this maze?" Cam asked. "Did either of you pay attention to how we came in?"

Hex shook her head, but Fuse grinned and pulled out a vial. "Lucky for you fools, I was—"

"All right, fine!" a goblin roared, and Fuse stuffed the vial back into her pocket. "We'll have it your way and start with the scrawny one tonight and save the juicier ones for the feast tomorrow." He threw open the cell door and scooped up Fuse in an enormous claw and slung her over his shoulder. "Come on. You need a good marinating."

Hex and Cam shouted and threw themselves at the goblin, but he brushed them aside as if they were little more than bugs. Hex fell to the floor in a sprawl and scrambled to her knees, only to be knocked down again by Cam slamming into her side. His head hit the wall with a thud.

Hex glanced up in time to see the goblin carrying Fuse away. Strangely, Fuse had stopped struggling. Instead of fighting, she was focused on dripping something from the glass vial she'd been trying to show them earlier. Then she was gone.

The last remaining goblin, a blocky, squat creature with a dangerous-looking sword strapped to her waist, locked the prison cell and stuck the key into her back pocket.

"Cam, are you okay?" Hex asked, crouching over him.

Cam blinked slowly and rubbed his head. "Mm-hmm." He nodded, but winced.

A dirty orange light permeated the cell, barely illuminating walls hewn directly into the stone. It looked like it had once been a storage closet, but someone had decided to renovate it by pulling out the shelves, leaving behind only a small pile of rusty nails and chunks of wood in the otherwise empty cell.

The squat goblin guarding them strolled by, patrolling the corridor.

"We've got to get out of here," Cam said. "We've got to save Fuse." His face was scrunched up, and Hex thought he might be about to cry.

"We will," Hex promised, even though she didn't have the foggiest idea how. "But we need to figure a way out of this. I'll think of a plan, but you need to help me with the clank."

Cam nodded, but his leg jiggled nervously and his eyes were wide and watery. He wouldn't be any use if he didn't calm down. Hex's stomach tightened. It was up to her to be the leader then.

"She means a lot to you, doesn't she?"

Cam nodded once—a sharp, definitive answer. "She's my best friend. She helped me when I was alone, when my dad abandoned me."

Hex touched his arm. "And now you're going to help her. But first I need *your* help. You remember that vial?"

Cam nodded.

Hex hoped she was right about what Fuse had been doing with the liquid in the vial. "Fuse left us a trail."

13

POSITIVELY MAGNETIC

"We need to bust out of here, and then we can follow Fuse's trail," Hex said. "My backpack is still in the car—do you have anything with you?"

"They took my vest," Cam said. "It has most of my mechanical parts. But I've still got a few things in my pants pockets." He pulled out a jumble of wires, some electronic components Hex recalled seeing in *The Curious Book of Clank*, and a small black spool.

"Sticky ribbon!" Hex exclaimed. "That stuff is great—I used it in Grundzilla's cave!"

"Oh, you mean tape?" Cam asked. "Yeah, it's useful stuff."

The goblin guarding their cell marched past again, the top of the key sticking tantalizingly out of her back pocket. Cam and Hex sat so they blocked the supplies from her view.

"If we can get her to face away from us for a few seconds, we might be able to get the key from her back pocket . . ." Hex grabbed a rusty iron nail and began scratching an image on the floor. She couldn't really see anything she drew in the dim light, but just the act of sketching helped. "Maybe we could make a hook to grab it from her pocket," Hex said, thinking about how she got bread from high shelves at the grocer's.

"She might notice if we accidentally poke her in the butt," Cam said. His posture was still uncharacteristically slumped, but his expression now was one of focus. This was clank, which was something he could do. Hex was counting on it. "It'd be nice if we could make something that just grabbed the key without actually touching her."

"Wasn't there something in the book about a thing that attracts metal?"

Cam's face broke out into a smile. "A magnet! Ace job, Hex!"

Hex felt an unexpected flush of warmth at the compliment. "So you have a magnet with you?"

"Sure, I've got a magnet in my vest pock—" Cam stopped with his hand hovering above a nonexistent pocket.

The warmth evaporated. "Guess it wasn't that great an idea after all."

"Hmm . . ." Cam nosed through the pile of clank, then flourished a battery and a coil of wire. "We can make an electromagnet!" Hex could almost see the weight of Cam's panic lifting, replaced with the crackle of his usual energy. "When you run electricity through a wound-up wire, it makes a magnetic pull. And it's even stronger when you wrap it around an iron core, like that nail you've got."

Cam took the nail and wound the wire around it tightly, then taped both ends to a large cylindrical battery from the pile of clank. He brought the contraption close to another nail on the floor. It popped off the ground and onto the electromagnet.

"Sparks! That's awesome!" Hex whispered. They waited for the guard to pass again, then they dug through the broken pieces of shelving and found several long slivers of wood. They taped them together to form a long pole and attached the electromagnet to the end of it. "We still need to figure out how to get the guard to stop long enough for us to grab the key."

"I've got an idea . . ." Cam searched through the electronics until he found a black cylinder the width of his thumbnail, with two short wires extending from one end. He taped two longer wires onto each of the short ones, then threw the cylinder out of the prison cell toward the opposite corridor wall, still holding the long wires like a leash. The cylinder lay hidden in the shadows outside their cell, the long wires snaking back through the bars and into Cam's hand. He stuck one wire to the coin battery. "You ready with that electromagnet?"

Hex nodded. "Sure, but what's that thing supposed to—"

Beeeeep.

The device emitted a high-pitched squeal as Cam brought the second wire in contact with the coin battery. The irritating sound drilled into Hex's skull.

"Electronic buzzer," Cam said with a grin.

"What is that brain-bleeding sound?" the guard demanded, marching toward them. Cam removed the wire from the battery when the goblin was only a yard away. The sound stopped instantly. She looked around, puzzled. "Were you making that noise?"

Cam and Hex shook their heads.

"Well, it's stopped now," the goblin said and began to walk away. *Beeeeeeeep.*

The goblin whipped around, her lip curled in furious bewilderment. She tilted an ear toward the ground and Cam threw the ends of the wires he was holding out of the cell so she couldn't trace them back to him. "It's coming from there," she muttered, and knelt down to look closer. Her crouched position made the top of the key stick out even farther from her pocket.

Hex pushed the magnet-on-a-stick through the bars of their cell, slowing when she was inches away from the goblin's expansive bottom. She held her breath and maneuvered the magnet closer, closer, closer . . .

"Oh, I found it!" the goblin shouted triumphantly.

Hex twitched the stick, and the key slipped out of the goblin's pocket and stuck right onto the magnet. She yanked the magnet-on-a-stick back through the bars of the cell and shoved it behind her just as the guard stood up and turned to face them.

The goblin brandished the buzzer and glared at them through

narrowed yellow eyes. "What kind of a thaum is this?"

Hex shrugged. "It's not ours. We can't do magic."

The goblin sniffed them, then the buzzer as if to confirm this. "Not a thaum," she mumbled. "Fine. You tell me if you see anything else like it."

"Without hesitation," Hex promised. The guard grunted and walked off to continue her patrol. Hex turned to Cam, beaming. "Let's find Fuse and get out of here."

Cam gathered everything back into his pockets. They waited until the guard was at the other end of the corridor, then Hex put her hand through the bars and unlocked the cell door. They slipped out and crept down the hallway away from the guard and in the direction the goblins had taken Fuse. It wasn't long before they reached a fork in the corridor.

"Aww, monkey wrench!" Cam cursed. "This place is a maze."

"The trail," Hex reminded Cam.

In unison, they looked at the rocky ground, almost invisible in the gloom. Cam took an LED and battery from his pocket, but even with the light, all they could see was stone floor. Nothing else.

Hex squatted on the ground and swept a hand over the floor. Her fingers brushed over a wet patch of stone. Cam lowered the light to where Hex crouched. She could see the faint glint of liquid. The path. Her heart sank—it would take forever to stop every few steps to search for an almost invisible patch of liquid. Even if the goblins took their time marinating Fuse, the liquid would dry up at this rate.

"Cam, what type of stuff would Fuse have in her pockets?" Hex had noticed the types of clank Fuse and Cam did were very different. Cam seemed to use a lot of what the book called electronics and mechanics, whereas Fuse's style of clank involved a lot more . . . explosions.

"She likes chemistry," Cam said. "She's got all kinds of chemicals with her, not just explosives."

The Curious Book of Clank mentioned chemistry, but only briefly. It said it was an entire field in itself and that readers should refer to other books. From what Hex gathered of the brief summary, it was a bit like the work her parents did at the apothecary, but using clank principles instead of magic to create concoctions.

Hex spun the beads on her necklace. The whole situation reminded her of a No Magic Girl story. Spanner had asked if he could be included as a character and Hex had agreed on the condition that he would help tell the story. In it, Spanner was held hostage by an evil troll king. No Magic Girl went to rescue him, only to discover that the troll king had hidden him at the center of a maze. Spanner had impressed Hex with his cleverness when he said he would leave a trail of Light thaums for No Magic Girl to follow.

"Cam, are there any chemicals that light up? Like . . . an LED, but liquid?"

Cam's brow furrowed, and Hex regretted asking such a silly question. Then his usual lopsided grin spread across his face. He pulled another LED from his pocket, and it lit a dim purple. "It's an ultraviolet LED," he explained and lowered it to the floor. Hex gasped. Ghostly blue droplets glowed under the ultraviolet light. "Fuse was experimenting with chemicals to make invisible ink for the last few weeks . . . she must have had some leftover tonic water in that vial. It didn't work out as ink, but—wow, Hex, how do you think of these things?"

Hex shrugged and smiled. "I'm a storyteller."

"You're a Clanksmith," Cam countered.

Hex paused, surprised. Was she a Clanksmith? She didn't feel like one . . .

"We should hurry," Cam said, reminding her that now wasn't the best time to worry about what she was or wasn't. "I don't think it glows once it dries up."

Fuse's splashes of tonic water led them through one corridor and into another. Hex was just thinking how lucky it was they hadn't run into any other goblins when she practically walked headlong into one. She recognized the head-to-toe green armor immediately. It was Bert, the goblin who'd (fortunately) refused to eat her ear.

Hex acted fast, wrapping a hand around the goblin's helmet and pressing over the mouth slit. It was a move she called the "Spanner is about to tattle on me and I need him to shut up" technique.

"There's one of you and two of us," Hex hissed at the wriggling goblin. He was strong, and Hex didn't think she could hold on for long.

"Yeah, but the goblin has a spear," Cam pointed out.

"Grab it!" Hex grunted.

"Oh, right," Cam said. "Sorry." Was he apologizing to the *goblin*?

"All right, Bert. I'm going to let go now but you have to promise not to scream or fight back."

Bert nodded and Hex released him cautiously, ready to seize him again if he shouted for help. Instead, he gagged and wiped the mouth slit on his helmet with his armored hand. "Disgusting! You just had to shove your hand into my mouth, didn't you?"

"But . . . you've got face armor!" Cam pointed out.

"And *you* have all kinds of human diseases!"

"—which is *exactly* why you don't want to eat us!" Hex cut in. "So how about you let us sneak by, and the chef will have to find something else for dinner—something that actually tastes good!"

"Hmm . . . appealing prospect," Bert said. "But I'd get in big trouble if anyone ever found out. I could lose my job."

"You can say that we ambushed you," Hex suggested.

"That might work . . . what do I get out of it?"

"You don't have to eat us," Hex said. "And we don't have to use this spear."

"Well . . . it would give the chef an excuse to try that new *boeuf flambé* recipe he's been telling me about. Oh, all right then. Could you tie me up so it looks like a real ambush?"

Hex looked Bert up and down. He was about her height and small-shouldered like she was. "Actually, that gives me an idea . . ."

"How do I look?" Hex asked, arms outspread. The green armor covered her almost completely—only her eyes were visible through a slit in the helmet.

"Scary," Cam said.

"Like you ambushed me and stole my armor," Bert grumbled. Underneath his armor, he was wearing a surprisingly dapper suit jacket and a nice leather belt, which Cam used to tie him up. "You may as well keep it. You've infected it now, I'm sure."

Hex tore off two strips of fabric from her dress for Cam to wrap around his own mouth and wrists so it looked like he was gagged and tied. Waving goodbye to Bert, she hefted the spear and walked behind Cam, pretending to prod him forward with its tip.

They continued this way down the corridor, occasionally stopping at junctions to discreetly check for more of Fuse's trail. The first time they passed a group of goblins, Hex was practically shaking in her armor as she marched Cam down the hallway, trying to look like she knew what she was doing. The other goblins nodded at her in greeting, and one of them remarked, "Another human roast for tonight, eh?"

Hex nodded, and Cam pretended to look scared. Or maybe

he wasn't pretending. To Hex's relief, the goblins let them pass and didn't seem the least bit suspicious. They crossed a few more goblins, but none of them seemed to notice anything awry. Hex was just starting to worry Fuse would run out of tonic water when her trail led them to a slightly open door with the scent of fried onions wafting out.

Hex and Cam peeked in to see a large cavern, well-lit by a roaring fire. An enormous goblin in a white apron and a tall chef's hat bustled around an equally enormous frying pan suspended over the fire, shaking in spices and stirring onions. To the left of the fire, an armored goblin stood guard by a stone pillar in the center of the room. Something—or someone—was tied to the pillar.

Hex leaned closer to get a better view and gulped. Bound, gagged, and smothered in brown marinade was the night's main entrée, *Fuse à la carte*.

14

CRÈME DE CLANKSMITH

Hex and Cam drew back into the shadows and exchanged wide-eyed looks.

"The onions are almost caramelized," the chef said. "What time did you say the king wanted dinner?"

"In an hour," said the guard.

"That's barcly enough time to cook the human," the chef grumbled. "It won't taste good anyway, since the marinade won't have soaked in properly."

"It's what the king wants."

"The king has an undiscerning palate. A *basilisk bourguignon* would be far nicer—it's got a lovely, complex texture with a broody, smoky finish."

"You sound like Bert," the guard grumbled. That gave Hex an idea. "Human is one of my favorite dishes."

"Wait here," Hex told Cam. "I got this."

Hex strode in with far more confidence than she felt, her eyes raking across the kitchen. The chef was still fussing about the pan, shaking in some pepper and glittering pixie dust. Spices, sauces, and a large stack of recipe books were cluttered atop the wooden table beside him. He clearly took his culinary endeavors seriously.

Hex approached the goblin who was standing guard over Fuse. "Your shift's over." She pitched her voice low and gruff like Bert's. "I'm on duty."

Her palms sweated; would the goblin see right through her ruse?

But the goblin visibly relaxed from his stiff stance. "Finally," he said. "Thanks, Bert. My shift started just as I got to the last chapter of *The Amorous Adventures of Amalda The Alchemist: Book Seven, Werewolf, Where Wolf.* I've been *dying* to know if Amalda figures out that the vampyre prynce is actually a werewolf." He scurried out.

Hex pretended to check Fuse's bindings. Fuse was gagged but her glare could have burned a hole through the wall—apparently she didn't recognize Hex with the armor.

"Ugh, why are we having human again?" Hex said to the chef.

"I know, I know," he grumbled. "You know how it is. The king and the other goblins love it. Bert, you and I are the only proper gourmands here. I keep trying to tell the king—fairy, chicken, griffin, tofu . . . Much easier to cook, and *far* more flavorful. Take a nice jackalope stew—it has beautiful aromatic undertones and a velvety consistency. With humans, it's all I can do just to cover up their blandness."

"Yeah," Hex agreed. "And they're greasy and unhealthy!" She took a few steps closer to the table, looking for something she could use. Her eye alighted on a bowl of thick red jelly. Perfect.

"Isn't that right?" The cook poured a prodigious amount of oil into the pan. "And they have hardly any nutritional value."

"I've heard they have all sorts of diseases," Hex said, hoping the chef read the same cooking magazines as Grundzilla. She waited until his back was turned and then grabbed the bowl of jelly.

"I know!" said the chef. "Nasty things, skulking about all day above ground! Who knows what kinds of germs they catch?"

The chef kept his back to Hex, his focus on the pan in front of him. Hex pulled off one of her armored gloves and dipped a finger into the jelly. Then she dabbed it in large red splotches on Fuse's face, wiping off the brown marinade so the red stood out better. Fuse threw her head from side to side, but Hex was relentless. After a minute, it looked like Fuse had some type of horrible spotty rash.

"Do you think they're contagious if we eat them?" Hex faked a nervous tremble in her voice.

"Could be, could be," the chef said. "I think I read about something in *Bone Appétit*. There's something going around, some kind of—"

"Rash?" Hex supplied. "Oh, yes, the—" What had Grundzilla called it? "The Red-Spotted Death. It's supposed to be really contagious. Horribly painful way to die." Hex pulled off her other glove and dabbed more of the jelly all over her hands. The gelatinous consistency made her hands look like they were covered in large, shiny pustules. "Almost always fatal," she added.

"I really need to talk to the king about this." The chef shook his head. "Well, I need to get this human sautéed. Untie it, will you?"

"Sure, I—" Hex paused for the barest fraction of a second to build up suspense. Then she threw back her head and shrieked at the top of her lungs.

The chef whipped around to see what was wrong. Then his gaze traveled right past Hex and landed on Fuse. His mouth dropped open in horror. Slowly, he raised a shaking hand and pointed at her. "The—the R-Red-Spotted Death!" he whispered.

Hex let out another cry. "My hands!" Hex wailed, trying to sound convincingly terrified. She flapped her hands frantically in the chef's face. "I've caught the disease!"

The chef released a bloodcurdling scream. He scrambled away from her, nearly running into the pan. "The Red-Spotted Death! You've doomed us all!" He ran out of the kitchen and down the hallway, hollering hysterically the entire way.

Hex grabbed a kitchen knife from the table and started to cut through Fuse's bonds. Fuse struggled, but Hex tipped up the helmet. "It's me!" she hissed. Fuse immediately relaxed, her eyes crinkling with relief.

"What did you do?" Cam asked as he entered the kitchen. "That chef was screaming about quarantining the entire lair." He spotted Fuse, then launched himself at her and wrapped her in a hug. "Fuse! Holy harmonic oscillator! What happened to your face?"

"Fuse and I have caught the deadly Red-Spotted Death!" Hex said as she finished sawing through Fuse's ropes.

Fuse pulled off her gag. "Better than being eaten."

"Well, I couldn't stand the idea of a goblin *gobblin'* you up," Hex said with a wink.

Fuse groaned. "Please stop."

"Nope."

"So what's the plan now?" Fuse asked. She rummaged around the chef's table. "I thought I saw the chef put it here . . ." she mumbled to herself. Then she pulled out Cam's lime green vest from behind the table. "Ta-da! The chef said he was saving it for a friend who loves this color. Blake or Bort or—"

"Bert!" Hex snapped up the vest. "That would be me, thank you!" The look of utter betrayal on Cam's face made Hex laugh and she handed him the vest. "Bert wouldn't have even touched it anyway."

Cam took it, delighted. "So how are we getting out of here?"

Hex grinned, lowered the helmet back over her face, and extended the bowl of red jelly to the Clanksmiths.

***

They exited the goblin cave thirty minutes and a lot of screaming later. The chef had already done half the work for them when he ran through the caverns shrieking about the Red-Spotted Death. All they needed to do was traipse through the halls, Hex in the lead with her armored disguise, shouting at the other goblins to run away, with Cam and Fuse following behind groaning hideously and flaunting their red-spotted hands and faces. Mass panic ensued, with goblins screeching and running as soon as they caught sight of the supposedly diseased humans. Not a single goblin tried to stop the Clanksmiths. In fact, they were quite useful in helping Hex, Cam, and Fuse navigate the labyrinthine caverns, usually by waving their hands wildly toward the exit and screaming "Get out! Get out!"

"That was fun!" Fuse laughed. "Next time any of those goblins gets so much as a zit, they're gonna panic about the Red-Spotted Death!"

Cam licked one of his hands. "This jelly isn't half bad either."

"Cam, that might be made from their last human captives," Hex said.

Cam lowered his hand, his eyes round and horrified.

"Naw, it tastes like raspberry," Fuse said, licking the spots from her fingers. "Shame we didn't stay for dessert."

A sliver of sun had begun to peep over the horizon. They found the car right where they left it, still blocked by the tree. Hex walked the length of the felled trunk, frowning. "How do we get this out of the way?" she asked, even as her mind started rigging up elaborate plans with ropes and pulleys.

"Remember that chemistry stuff I mentioned earlier?" Cam asked.

A downright wicked grin spread wide across Fuse's face as she completed Cam's thought. "I think it's time for a live demo . . . "

15

ONCE A PUN A TIME

"Hex? Hex, you all right?" Hex vaguely registered Cam waving a hand in front of her face.

"Fuse *blew up* the tree," she muttered.

"Yes, I did!" said Fuse gleefully.

They'd been driving for a little while now and were almost out of the mountains, but Hex still wasn't over her shock. "It just blew in half! Boom! Tree bits, everywhere!"

"I know, wasn't it just wonderful?" Fuse replied.

"No wonder you guys hide clank from ordinary people," Hex said, shaking her head slowly. "Is stuff like this normal in Clank City?"

"Yep," Fuse said. "Like, there's this fountain that shoots fire out every hour, just for fun. The clank we brought with us is stuff we can easily hide or disguise as magic. But in Clank City, we don't need to hide anything. There's buildings covered in solar panels and wind turbines to make electricity, and machines that can cut with lasers, and robots that fly. And no one looks down on you or

144

calls you a Mooch 'cause you can't do magic."

"And there's a school that teaches clank instead of magic! That's where *The Curious Book of Clank* is from," Cam added, his face bright with excitement. "They don't care if you're Undeveloped or Developed as long as you want to learn. That's the best part—you've got to be born with magic, but anyone can learn clank!"

"You have to chip in and work," Fuse continued. "But they took care of me and Cam even though we didn't have any money."

"Work?" Hex asked, recalling her humiliating attempt to get a job with Mr. Bobbin. "They let Undeveloped people work?"

"Of course!" Cam laughed. "How else would we get stuff done?"

Work. And school! Like a regular kid. If she went to Clank City, no one would care that she couldn't do magic. She could support herself and not be a burden on her—

Her *family*. What was she thinking? She couldn't just abandon them—abandon Spanner—to go live in some faraway city.

"Well . . . this'll make some story for my brother," she said, trying to change the subject. She didn't want to talk about Clank City anymore, how wonderful it might be, and how far from home it was.

"Is he Undeveloped also?" Cam asked.

"No, he's normal. Although I don't think he really realizes being Undeveloped *isn't* normal," Hex said. Until she'd met the Clanksmiths, Spanner was the only person who hadn't treated her with a measure of pity or discomfort. He had been born around the time Hex had been diagnosed as Undeveloped and had never known her as anything but. To Spanner, her lack of magic was just one of her many characteristics; there was nothing wrong or unusual about it. "I draw pictures and tell him stories about this girl who can't do magic, and I think they've gone to his head."

"Oh, like those the pictures you showed me when we first met?" Cam asked.

Hex chuckled uncomfortably, somewhat embarrassed she'd brought up her stories at all. "Yeah, those."

"Will you tell us one?"

"They're just kids' stories . . ." Hex protested.

"It's still hours to Midbar," Fuse said. "It's stories or listening to Cam's snoring."

"No, really, they're silly," Hex said, waving her hand dismissively. "I shouldn't have said anything."

"Please?" Cam asked in a plaintive tone so like Spanner's, Hex was taken aback.

"Sure . . . I guess." Hex took a deep breath, and started her story. "Once upon a time, there was a girl different from all the other kids. They could make fairies sleep with a wave of their hands or make goblins dance uncontrollably with only a word. This girl couldn't do any of those things. She didn't need to, because she could pull an idea out of thin air and use her imagination to make it a reality. This girl was No Magic Girl."

Fuse muffled a snort, and Hex stopped, feeling even more embarrassed than before. "I told you, they're just silly stories," she muttered.

"I want to hear it," Cam said, his eyes boring into her with genuine longing. There was something deeper there—something more than just the desire to hear a story. Hex didn't know what it was, but it was enough to persuade her to continue.

She opened her mouth, intending to tell one of Spanner's favorite stories, then hesitated. When she finally continued, she found herself spinning an entirely new story that included what she'd seen and learned about clank in the past few days.

Spanner would like this story. In it, No Magic Girl faced an evil dragon to save her town. "No weapon could penetrate the beast's thick hide, so the town used all its thaumium to keep the dragon at bay," Hex said. "But they could only hold the dragon off for so long. Their thaumium burned out, and the dragon broke through every enchantment, spell, and ward."

As the words wove around them, Hex felt more and more comfortable in her telling. Cam leaned toward her, his eyes drinking in her words. Fuse, despite her initial skepticism, listened with a faint smile on her face.

"The townspeople were at a loss. None of them knew what to do—except for No Magic Girl. She'd learned to rely on her wits instead of thaumium and magic. So she decided to build a, um . . . machine? A machine to stop the dragon. A flying robot like they have in Clank City." Hex broke off. "Cam, can you help me with this part? I don't actually know what a robot is."

Cam gave a small shake of his head, breaking out of his reverie. "Oh. Um. A robot's a machine that can do stuff automatically. We've got all kinds, ones that drive like my go-cart, some that fly, and even a few that kinda look like people. There's these flying ones in Clank City called quadcopters you can control with a remote, or even make them go by themselves."

"No Magic Girl built a quadcopter. It was about the size of . . ." Hex glanced at Cam, who held his hands out to demonstrate. "The size of a cat. It could fly, even without a Levitation spell."

"But with a Levitation spell, you can only float things up," Cam added, smiling proudly. "A quadcopter has four motors with propellers, and it can go up, down, side to side."

Hex nodded and continued, weaving this new information into her story. "The quadcopter could fly with the agility of a hummingbird. She flew it right at the dragon's giant head. The dragon roared and tried swatting it away like it was an annoying pixie. At the last moment, No Magic Girl maneuvered the quadcopter away from the dragon's enormous claw. She flew it around its head in circles. The dragon spun, snapping, biting, and clawing at it."

As she told the story, Hex's heart surged. She missed Spanner so badly it hurt. She could imagine him here with them, his eyes alight with excitement at hearing a new story, laughing and gasping at all the right parts. Did he feel like she'd abandoned him?

"Round and round and round the dragon went, so irritated by No Magic Girl's quadcopter it didn't even notice when it started to get dizzy, then to wobble. Green from nausea, it staggered and flapped its gigantic wings to try to keep its balance. It teetered and tottered until finally, it fell over with a humongous crash. 'I have never before been defeated! What kind of magic is this?' the dragon croaked.

"'Magic? Who needs magic?' No Magic Girl said. 'I'll let you go, but you have to promise you'll never bother us again.' The dragon promised, and once it was no longer dizzy, it flew away, leaving behind a gigantic pile of treasure," Hex finished.

"No wonder you've got such a knack for clank," Fuse said.

Cam nodded in agreement. "My brother would like that story." He didn't sound like his usual excited self when he spoke. He was looking past Hex into the distance, his gaze unfocused.

"You must really miss him," Hex said, thinking of her own brother. "Don't worry—we're going to kick the Thunder Knight's butt, and you'll be back in Clank City before you know it! Then you'll have all kinds of new stories to tell your brother." And she could go back to Spanner, an ordinary, magical person.

Cam's forehead scrunched up uncertainly. "I'm . . . going to take a nap." He rested his head back against the seat and turned away from Hex.

She climbed over into the front seat next to Fuse and waited for Cam's ragged breaths to even out. It was a long time before Hex was sure he was actually asleep. Finally, she leaned toward Fuse and whispered, "Did I say something wrong?"

Fuse glanced away from the road. "Cam hasn't actually seen his brother in almost four years."

"What?" Hex exclaimed. "But he talks about him all the time!"

"His father gave Cam up to an orphanage right after his mom died and she couldn't protect him anymore. His dad kept his Developed little brother. Cam's been trying to track them down for years now."

Hex huffed in disgust, even though she knew it wasn't at all unusual for Undeveloped children to be abandoned. She was lucky—her parents loved her, and they would never give her up no matter how much of a burden she was.

"How did Cam get from an orphanage to Clank City?"

"He ran away looking for his dad and brother and wound up on the streets in the city of Runemont. That's how I met him. I was one of a few Undeveloped kids in my gang, so I tried to help Cam out. A few months after he joined, he got caught trying to pick this lady's pocket. Cam, good-hearted fool he is, burst into tears and apologized instead of running. Lucky for him, the lady was a traveler from Clank City, and when she learned his story, she brought him home with her." Cam stirred and Fuse darted a look back at him, but he didn't wake up.

They drove in silence for a long time, and finally Fuse told Hex to go to sleep. It was midday, but they hadn't slept the night before. "I'll wake up Cam when I'm too tired to drive."

Despite her exhaustion, Hex couldn't fall asleep. She thought about her truce with the Clanksmiths—they would work together only until they defeated the Thunder Knight. They hadn't seen that backstabbing bully since their escape from the fairies, but the closer they drew to the Wyrm, the more likely they were to run into him. And that meant her time with the Clanksmiths was coming to an end.

Instead of being excited about the possibility of finding the Wyrm, Hex just felt sick. She couldn't even muster enough fear for whatever obstacles lay ahead in the Great Barren. She was scared for what came *after*. In the brief time she'd known them, the Clanksmiths had become her friends. If she made it to the Wishing Wyrm first, could she take Cam's wish from him? She had to. She couldn't go back to Spanner and her family a failure.

Hex pretended to be asleep when Fuse pulled the car over a few hours later and shook Cam awake. Night had fallen, and still Hex couldn't sleep. Finally, she opened her eyes and sat up. Cam took his eyes off the road briefly to glance at her.

"Can't sleep?" he asked.

"No," Hex said. "Cam . . . I'm sorry about your brother. I didn't know . . ."

"It's okay. It's my fault I didn't tell you earlier."

From the moment she'd met him, Cam had been filled with a frenetic, cheerful energy. But the boy sitting next to her now sat completely still, his breaths long and slow, a worried furrow between his brows. She wasn't sure why, but she put her hand on top of his. He took it off the wheel and slipped it into hers without hesitation. It wasn't a romantic gesture; he clutched her hand like it was an anchor.

They sat in thoughtful silence, driving through an endless, desolate dome of stars. It was a while before Hex spoke again.

"Cam, no matter what happens, we'll still be friends, right?"

He smiled. It was a shadow of his usual lopsided grin, but even that was enough to make his face light up. "Yeah. Definitely."

"Can I ask you . . . what's your wish?"

She'd been burning with curiosity to know since Fuse had revealed that Cam's wish wasn't to be normal, but she hadn't asked. At first, it was because she was too angry at the Clanksmiths to admit she wanted to know. Then it was because she didn't *want* to care—they were rivals, right? But now . . . now she knew if she got her wish, it meant Cam wouldn't get his, which was the difficult truth that kept her from falling asleep.

Cam didn't immediately reply. "Do I have to tell you?"

Hex blinked, a little surprised. Cam was so honest and open, it hadn't occurred to her it was a secret he wanted to keep. She'd assumed it was Fuse who insisted on being cagey. If she pressed Cam, he would probably tell her, but she didn't want to force him. "No, that's all right."

She felt his hand relax in hers. "I'm sorry. It's just . . ." He let out a long sigh, then turned to her with a melancholy smile. "Hex, when this is all done, will you come to Clank City with us?"

Hex hesitated. She thought again about what Cam had said about going to school and working in Clank City; how both his and Fuse's faces brightened when they talked about home.

"I can't leave my little brother," she said finally.

"I thought you might say that," Cam said. His eyes slipped off of her, and he nodded distantly to himself. "If I ever find my brother, I'm never leaving him either."

16

WE'RE COOL 'CAUSE WE'RE FANS

"There's Midbar, the last bit of civilization before the Great Barren!" Fuse announced. The sun had risen and the mountains had given way to an arid landscape. In the distance, the houses of Midbar sat low and squat, built out of brownish yellow clay. And surrounding the town . . .

Hex squinted, then frowned. "There's a whole bunch of carriages, tents, horses, and what might be a giant bear . . ."

Fuse stopped the car and unfolded a map. "The other roads from the west join up at Midbar. Those must be wish hunters. Midbar's kind of in the middle of nowhere so everyone probably got here around the same time."

"Then there's going to be lots of fighting." Hex sighed. "Are there any other ways into the Great Barren?"

"Not unless you want to drive another few hundred miles south," Fuse said. "The whole desert is surrounded by cliffs, and Midbar's the closest place with a road that goes down into it."

There was a rumble, and as they watched, a black cloud coalesced above the town, punctuating the endless blue sky of the desert. It flashed as threads of lightning crackled through it, followed by thunderclaps.

"Aw, lug nuts," Cam said. "Looks like the Thunder Knight beat us to Midbar."

"Don't look so disappointed," Hex said. "He's keeping the other wish hunters busy!"

"Doesn't that include us?" Cam asked.

"Not if he doesn't recognize us!" Hex pointed at a far-off wagon. A sloppily painted thunderbolt surrounded by hearts adorned the side of it. "Those aren't all wish hunters."

Fuse followed Hex's gaze and gagged. "Ugh, fans. Even worse."

"Well, you'll have to pretend for just a little bit," Hex grinned.

***

"Do we have to wear these?" Fuse asked, and Hex flinched back. It was a little disconcerting to see Fuse's dark eyes gleaming out from the paper mask with the Thunder Knight's face drawn on. Hex had drawn one for each of them using colored pencils Cam had dug up from the trunk in the back of the car. Luckily, Hex had years of practice drawing the Thunder Knight . . . but she wasn't going to let Cam or Fuse know that.

"Any better ideas to keep him from recognizing us?" Hex asked as she tied down her hair. Even with the mask, her dandelion puff of black curls was too distinctive. Fuse had jammed a hat over her

155

turquoise hair to hide it as well.

"Please, he's way too self-absorbed to remember what we look like," Fuse scoffed, but she didn't take off the mask. "Why do you have this thing anyway?" She pointed at the "I've been Thunderstruck!" pin that Hex had given her to wear on her overalls. Hex had never quite gotten around to throwing it away.

"Um . . ." Hex felt her cheeks get warm.

"No. *No way*. I knew you liked the Thunder Knight, but you're a *Thunderhead*?" Fuse's expression was a mixture of amused incredulity and evil glee.

"I *was* a Thunderhead. Before I knew he was an arrogant double-crossing liar!"

"Did you write him letters? Put posters of him by your bed? I'll bet you even got the fan magazine! Sparks, this is *too* good!"

"The magazine subscription was a birthday present! I'm going to cancel it when I get home! Are you even listening? Fuse, stop laughing!" Hex tried to muster whatever scraps of dignity she had left before facing Cam. "Cam, is the potato . . . thing ready?" Hex asked.

Cam patted the clank device on the seat next to him. It was a long white tube with a thicker, shorter tube curved underneath, forming an uneven "U" shape. "I'll pump the potato cannon up when we're close."

Hex slid on her own mask. "Let's do this thing."

They rolled into town with the car's canopy down, cheering and hollering, "Thunder Knight!" and "Ra! Ra! Ra!" Cam waved a flag with a heart encircling a thunderbolt while Hex and Fuse threw handfuls of shredded paper confetti into the air.

"Welcome, fellow Thunderheads!" A girl with silky black hair waved at them. "I love your masks! Did you make them?"

"I did, thank you! I just *love* the Thunder Knight!" Hex gushed. Fuse slowed the car so the girl could walk alongside them. "What happened here?" She waved a hand at the scorch marks scarring the ground and the frazzled wish hunters who were only just getting back onto their feet.

"Oh my sparks! It was *AMAZING*!" the girl shouted. "The Thunder Knight came in and just like, *DESTROYED* the other wish hunters. He was all like, *ZAP*! *ZAP*! *ZAP*! and they just had to run for it!"

"Wow! Amazing!" Hex replied. "Where is he now? I *reeeeeally* want his autograph!"

"He went into town! That's where I'm going now!"

"Thank you!" Hex said, and they drove slowly into the town. It was chaos. Things were on fire, people were incapacitated by Stop spells, Dream spells, Upside-Down spells. One wish hunter on the main street spun like a top, out of control—Hex didn't even recognize that spell. A horse whinnied, its hind legs encased in purple goo. And everywhere, the Thunder Knight's tell-tale scorch marks stained the road in black blasts. Townspeople and fans alike peered through windows and lined the roads to watch the spectacle, some subdued with fear or wide-eyed with curiosity, others openly cheering for the Thunder Knight. Defeated wish hunters watched with slumped shoulders and sorrowful faces.

"Go Thunder Knight . . ." Cam said, barely above a whisper.

"This place is a mess," Fuse muttered. She started to turn the car around a corner, then abruptly hit the brakes and backed up.

"What's wrong?" Hex asked.

Fuse pressed a finger to her lips, then motioned for Hex and Cam to follow her out of the car. "Look," she whispered, ducking behind a sand-colored building.

Hex poked her head around the corner of the building, then shrank back immediately. The Thunder Knight stood in the middle of the road, a gaggle of adoring fans surrounding him.

"Young lady, your sacrifice will be remembered throughout history!" the Thunder Knight boomed, and Hex peeked around the corner again. A small girl with a red ribbon in hand stood dwarfed by the Thunder Knight's hulking presence. Hex gaped as she traced the ribbon to the collar of an enormous lion. He was so big that with his golden fur he looked like another of the yellow clay buildings.

"I don't want to be remembered for my sacrifice!" the girl said in a small, quavering voice. She looked Spanner's age. "I just want Mr. Sandy Paws!"

The lion growled, and the scattered grains of sand blown in from the desert floated and swirled toward him as though carried by an invisible wind.

"That's a sand lion," Hex breathed, her mind flashing back to one of Spanner's picture books, *Beasts of the Desert*. There'd been a lot of illustrations of cute rodents with cacti sprouting from their backs and lizards with hard sandstone hides, but Spanner's favorite animal had always been the sand lion. He'd spent the entire week after getting the book drawing pictures of scribbly lions with the clouds of sand they trailed behind them when they ran. It was also one of the very few animals that could travel through a desert as large as the Great Barren safely.

"Mr. Sandy—what sort of a name is that for such a majestic creature?" The Thunder Knight threw back his head and laughed. His fans crowed along with him and the girl shrank into herself. "I will pay for your lion in gold and silver and care for him well. Now wouldn't you like that?"

"No!" the girl said, her face screwed up like she was about to cry. "You can't have him!"

The crowd shifted uncomfortably—the Thunder Knight wasn't supposed to make little kids cry.

He seemed to realize how bad this looked because he smiled and knelt by the girl, patting her on the head paternally. He whispered something into her ear, then he stood up and lifted her onto his shoulders. She waved at the crowd and they cheered, but Hex recognized the brittle smile that comes right before a flood of tears.

"Dear child, thank you for your assistance on my noble quest! I will train your lion well and make you the richest child in all of Midbar!" He gently placed her on the ground and then vaulted onto the lion's back, flourishing his sword. "Onward, Mr. Sandy Paws! Let us make your friend proud!"

Mr. Sandy Paws hesitated, turning back to look at his small human friend. She gave him a tight nod. The lion whimpered, then loped down the street, with the Thunder Knight's entourage chasing behind and cheering. No one seemed to notice the little girl standing alone in the now empty street, tears dripping down her cheeks.

Hex ran to her before she could stop herself, every sisterly bone in her body screaming to help. "It's going to be okay," she said, taking the girl's hands in her own.

"He—he said he'd strike Mr. Sandy Paws with lightning if I didn't do what he said," the girl sobbed. "Will Mr. Sandy Paws be all right?"

"He will be," Hex said, "We'll get him back to you, okay?"

The girl sniffled, but she nodded. "My name is Ari. Tell Mr. Sandy Paws you're my friend and he won't hurt you."

"The Thunder Knight is horrible!" Cam said, his fists tight. He looked angrier than Hex had ever seen him. "I can't believe I used to look up to him!"

"I did too," Hex muttered.

"Hang in there, Ari," Fuse said. "Come on guys, we gotta keep moving." Hex nodded, and squeezed Ari's small hands before standing.

They climbed back into the car and followed the procession of Thunder Knight fans and curious townspeople through Midbar and out the other side of the town. Even most of the defeated wish hunters straggled along to watch the spectacle. No one seemed to want to miss this historic moment.

The town was seated at the lip of a cliff above the desert; two hundred feet below them, the Great Barren stretched out, an unforgiving landscape of stone and sand that went on for miles. The only way down was a single curved ramp that hugged the side of the cliff.

"It's huge," Hex whispered. She felt like such a fool for having run away from home thinking she could safely cross this desert alone without a plan. Somewhere in the dead center, the Wishing Wyrm waited in the heart of its volcano.

If the outskirts of Midbar had been chaotic, then the entry to the desert was a veritable war zone. The lip of the inclined road where the Great Barren—and the curse—started was absolute madness. Abandoned carriages marked the invisible border where human magic and thaums stopped working. The wish hunters who hadn't been defeated by the Thunder Knight were locked in battle, screaming furious incantations and casting spells left and right.

Anyone who made it across the threshold into the desert found themselves suddenly defenseless against the spells hurled across the border. One woman managed to climb over a carriage and onto the ramp only to get both her feet stuck to the ground. Another hunter reflexively cast a Shield spell against a fireball, and looked shocked when the Shield never appeared and his hat caught on fire. Those few who had made any progress were attempting a futile trek on foot. Some hunters had brought horses and other riding animals— Hex even spotted a small woman atop a griffin—but their mounts were panicking in the fray.

The Thunder Knight stopped before the mess of hunters and calmly stretched out his hands in front of him. Blue-white light gathered in a crackling, growing mass in front of his palms. The other wish hunters didn't notice him until the first bolts of lightning struck through the middle of the crowd. *BOOM! BOOM!* People shrieked and rushed to cast Shield spells. It was over in minutes— the wish hunters who weren't knocked unconscious surrendered to the Thunder Knight's superior power. They parted to let him through, and the Clanksmiths followed in the procession. They drove slowly but steadily, moving closer and closer to the front of the crowd until they were practically behind the knight.

The Thunder Knight stopped at the edge of the cliff and faced his fans. He raised his sword in the air with one hand and held the other hand under his chin in an Amplify spell.

"Fellow wish hunters!" His magically amplified voice boomed over the cheering of the crowd. "Do not be disappointed or discouraged. My victory is not your failure! By contributing to my ascension to eternal life, you have guaranteed the world a hero who will protect the weak and innocent for eternity! You are witnessing history—a new era in which good triumphs over evil!"

"Sparks, will he ever *shut up*?" Fuse moaned.

The fans roared and cheered, and even some of the wish hunters applauded. Hex wanted to yell at them all to stop, to tell them all what a phony, selfish man the Thunder Knight really was. Next to her, Fuse flicked her lighter on and off with an expression of pure hatred on her face, and Cam glared at him with stony fury.

"When I return," the Thunder Knight bellowed, "I will return *immortal*!"

Hex clenched her fists. "Not if we can help it."

Cam readied the potato cannon using a small air pump. They watched as the Thunder Knight turned his stolen steed around and sped down the ramp, Mr. Sandy Paws kicking up a trail of dust as they entered the desert. The Clanksmiths waited until the Thunder Knight was well beyond the border where the curse started and he couldn't summon bolts of lightning. Then Hex turned to Fuse, and gave her a tight nod.

"Let's do this."

The car burst forward and flew down the ramp, Fuse zigzagging wildly to avoid the few remaining wish hunters trudging wearily back to Midbar. The cheers from the crowd deteriorated into confused muttering and then a bewildered hush. Hex imagined what they must be thinking—who would dare take on the Thunder Knight? And how was their carriage still working in the desert?

They drove so fast, the rush of air ripped off Hex's paper mask. They were right behind the Thunder Knight. He glanced over his shoulder, and Hex had only the briefest glimpse of him gaping flabbergasted. Whether it was because he recognized them or was bewildered that their "Spin thaums" still worked, she didn't know, but it was a very gratifying sight. Then they were past him, the sands rolling beneath them in a yellow blur.

"We did it!" Hex cheered as the car flew through the flat desert sands. "We're on our way to the Wishing—"

Her blood ran cold. *We work together until we get the Thunder Knight out of the way.*

"I'm not backstabbing you just yet," Fuse said through gritted teeth. "Look behind you."

Mr. Sandy Paws came at them with terrifying speed, sand flowing out behind him like an enormous cape. The Thunder Knight sat astride the lion's giant back, sword raised, a razor smile across his smug face.

"Drive faster!" Cam shouted.

"Thanks, Cam. I hadn't thought of that already," Fuse replied.

"You're doing that sarcasm thing again, right?"

"Noooo, Cam. Sarcasm? Under such dire circumstances? I would *never*."

"Why, hello again, children!" the Thunder Knight boomed, now keeping pace with them. "I see you freed yourselves from the fairies even without my help!"

"Excuse me?" Hex demanded. "We saved *you*! You're the one who betrayed us!"

"Some knight you are!" Cam added.

"Children, children," the Thunder Knight said with an indulgent smile, "I wouldn't expect you to understand."

"Mr. Sandy Paws, you don't have to do this!" Hex shouted.

"I'm afraid he does if he doesn't want his little lady hurt!" the Thunder Knight retorted. The lion made a small growling sound in the back of his throat and looked almost regretful. "What type of mysterious thaums are you using that make your carriage work in this accursed desert?"

"Like we'd tell you," Hex said. "Cam, now!"

Cam heaved the potato cannon over his shoulder, and Fuse slowed the car just enough for Cam to take aim. "Eat this!" he shouted, and a potato shot out of the cannon with a loud *fwoop*. It careened toward the Thunder Knight faster than Hex had thought possible for a potato. Just as it was about to hit, the sand flowed around Mr. Sandy Paws and the Thunder Knight, enveloping them completely. There was a buzzing sound, and the potato fell to the ground in thousands of minuscule pieces, shredded by the grains of sand.

"Nice try, but just because I can't do magic here doesn't mean my lovely steed can't." The Thunder Knight barked a laugh. "The curse only works on humans, remember?"

Hex, Cam, and Fuse stared at the remains of the potato.

"DRIVE DRIVE DRIVE!" Cam shouted.

Mr. Sandy Paws lunged at the moving car with a roar. Hex shrieked and yanked Cam backward as the beast got his massive paws over the door of the car. The Thunder Knight grabbed Cam's vest, and before Hex could stop him, he dragged Cam out of the car.

"Let go!" Cam screamed, pounding ineffectively at the knight's armored chest.

"Cam!" Hex shouted, and Fuse swung the car so they faced Mr. Sandy Paws. Hex stood up in her seat and took a swing at the Thunder Knight with the empty potato cannon. He blocked it easily with his sword.

"Turn back," the Thunder Knight growled. He shook Cam. "Or your friend gets it."

The lion veered away from the car, sand flowing around his body. Fuse spun the steering wheel, frantically trying to change their course, but the car had barely turned when the cloud of sand shot toward them. Hex felt a spike of terror as sand and wind engulfed the car like a monstrous hand. She tried to pull her goggles on, but the sand was already everywhere. She threw one arm over her eyes, trying to protect them, and grabbed Fuse with her other.

There was another roar and a colossal gust of wind. Then they were in the heart of the sandstorm. Fuse's hand ripped out of Hex's as the wind tossed them into the air. Hex hit the ground hard and blacked out.

17

LONG SCHEMES AND SHORT CIRCUITS

"Wake up! Hex!" A hand brushed at Hex's face, dislodging sand from her eyelids and nose.

"I'm awa—" Hex started to say, then spit as sand fell into her mouth. Fuse peered into Hex's face, with an expression so intense that Hex flinched back.

"Come on," Fuse said, dragging Hex up. "The Thunder Knight has Cam."

Hex leapt to her feet. "You didn't get him back?"

Fuse grimaced and shook her head, dropping her gaze.

"It's not your fault. We'll save him." Hex clenched her fists and snarled. "The Thunder Knight is going *down*."

They got into the car, which had taken a beating from their encounter with the Thunder Knight. The seats were ripped where Mr. Sandy Paws had grabbed the car, and one of the sides was dented, but the motor started up just fine.

Fuse unfolded the map and took out a round metal device

that fit in the palm of her hand. She moved it this way and that, studying it.

"What's that?" Hex asked.

"It's a compass," Fuse explained. "The Wishing Wyrm's volcano is in the center of the desert, but I need the compass to orient us." She looked down at the compass, then pointed. "That way."

Hex squinted and saw a small sandy-colored smudge on the horizon where Fuse had pointed. "I can see Mr. Sandy Paws' sand cloud. Looks like he already knows which way to go."

"Great," Fuse said, but her shoulders were bunched tight and Hex knew she was more worried than she let on. She put the compass and map away and started driving. "We need a plan if we're gonna get Cam back safely. We can't get close enough for the Thunder Knight to see us or he'll hurt him."

"We'll have to wait until they stop so we can sneak close," Hex said.

"Yeah, but they probably won't stop until they're at the volcano . . . and once we get there, the Thunder Knight'll have magic again."

"I know." Hex sighed. She hoped the legend about magic being even more powerful when the curse broke wasn't true. "I . . . have some ideas, but I need time to think."

Fuse nodded and didn't ask any further questions. Hex took it as a sign that Fuse had faith in her ability to come up with a good plan. The weight of responsibility settled on her, but also something else—a glimmer of pride. Here was something she was good at, and Fuse not only acknowledged it, but trusted her.

Hex pulled out her sketchbook as Fuse drove. She flipped to a blank page and froze. Someone had taped a folded piece of paper to the inside of her sketchbook. The handwriting was messy but legible. *Don't open until you're alone. —Cam*

Until you're alone. In other words—when they parted ways as rivals for the wish. Hex started to unfold it anyway, then stopped herself. Cam must have had a good reason for wanting her to wait. She needed to focus first on the plan to defeat the Thunder Knight and get Cam back.

Hex turned to the next blank page and started drawing. "He always uses that annoying Lightning spell . . ." she mused out loud, trying to push aside the thought of Cam's note. "Is there some way we can, I don't know, redirect the lightning back at him?"

"I dunno. It's magic, so who even knows if it follows the laws of physics? I mean, scientifically, you'd think it'd electrocute him."

"What's electrocute?"

"You know like—*ZAP!* Like when someone gets hit by lightning. Lightning's just electricity."

"What, really?" Hex gaped. "But—I thought the book said electricity is what you use to power LEDs and motors and stuff."

"It is. It's also lightning. The difference is that the amount of electricity going through an LED isn't gonna hurt you, but the amount in lightning will. So the Thunder Knight *shouldn't* be able to shoot it from his hands without zapping himself but . . . eh, who knows with magic."

"Well . . . it doesn't really touch him," Hex said slowly. "I've seen him do the spell a few times now. It doesn't come directly out of his hands. The electricity kind of . . . gathers and floats in front of them."

"Huh . . . " Fuse cocked her head. "So he doesn't get zapped because he's not really a part of the circuit."

"A circuit?" Hex asked.

"This is more Cam's thing than mine, but a circuit is a path that electricity travels on. Like with an LED and battery. If you pull the wire away from the battery, it stops working 'cause the electricity stops flowing. It's kind of the same with the Thunder Knight. The electricity doesn't go between his hands and the lightning because he's not actually connected to the circuit."

"So what happens if we close the circuit between the lightning and his body?" Hex asked.

Fuse's eyes went round, and then a slow, wicked grin spread across her face.

They drove for hours without a sign of any living creature other than the distant puff of sand marking Mr. Sandy Paws' position. Hex explained her plan to Fuse, then started on preparations. Throughout the day and into the evening, they drew closer but kept back far enough so the Thunder Knight wouldn't see or hear them.

"What if we don't make it before they get to the Wishing Wyrm's volcano?" Hex asked. She'd spent the last few hours building the clank they'd need for their plan, with Fuse chipping in instructions as she drove.

"The volcano is almost half a day's drive away and we're moving faster than Mr. Sandy Paws," Fuse said. "At this rate we'll catch up to them." Hex bit her lip. "It's not like Cam's going to knock out the Thunder Knight on his own and get to the wish first, if that's what you're worried about."

"That's not—I'm not worried about Cam getting the wish. It's the Thunder Knight I'm worried about!"

Fuse shrugged. "Just sayin'."

Her words stung. After everything they'd been through, Hex had almost forgotten they were still rivals. But Fuse hadn't forgotten. She wasn't here to help Hex or even be her friend. She was here to make sure Cam got the wish.

"Why is it so important to you that Cam gets his wish?" Hex asked. Fuse's eyes flashed, and Hex quickly clarified. "I mean—I understand why you want him to get the wish instead of me. I just meant, why did you want to help him in the first place? Most people would want the wish for themselves."

Fuse didn't answer for a minute. "I don't need the wish. Cam does. And I get what you're saying—a lot of people wouldn't go on a dangerous quest even to help out a friend." Fuse paused again, like she was debating how much to say. "Thing is . . . I'd do anything for Cam. He's my best friend, but it's more than just that. Cam gave me a life by introducing me to clank. I owe him . . . everything. This quest was *my* idea, not his. He doesn't ask for much for himself, you know? He's not that kind of person."

Hex nodded slowly. She hadn't known Cam for very long, but she understood what Fuse meant.

"I told you I helped Cam when he was on the streets. But I didn't tell you he helped me out too." Fuse smiled. "Wasn't long after he got to Clank City, Cam came back to convince me to come with him. He saw how life-changing clank was and knew he could help me. That's why he wanted to teach you clank also."

Hex twitched a smile at that.

"I'm sorry I said your wish was stupid." It took Hex a moment to remember what Fuse was talking about. "It wasn't fair. Before I met Cam, I would've given anything to be normal. Going to Clank City was easy for me—I wasn't leaving anyone behind. It's different for you. You've got a family who loves you and a little brother who looks up to you." Fuse took a deep breath and faced Hex. Her eyes blazed with a fierce inner fire. "But I will do *anything* for Cam."

Hex nodded solemnly. She understood. They were rivals. But that didn't mean Fuse wasn't also her friend.

18

WHO TURNED OFF THE LIGHTS?

They drove all night, keeping the car's headlights off so the Thunder Knight wouldn't spot them. The full moon bathed the desert in a glow bright enough to follow the sand cloud from Mr. Sandy Paws.

"Hex, is it just me, or is it getting darker?"

Hex blinked open heavy eyelids. She'd been nodding off, lulled by the hum of the car and the starlit sky rolling above. She looked up at the moon, then squinted. It looked like someone had hung a thin black veil in the sky—the bright orb still hung pale and white, but even as she watched, its light seemed to get dimmer and dimmer. But there wasn't a cloud in the sky, and even if the Thunder Knight was nearby, he couldn't cast any spells. There was only one creature that brought blackness darker than night.

An icy chill spread through Hex's chest even as Fuse slowed the car to a crawl, then stopped.

"Fuse, you don't think—"

Fuse's mouth twisted and she nodded. "'Fraid so."

"But there's nothing in the legends about Shades!" Hex protested, as if complaining would make the problem go away.

"Maybe they appeared in the hundred years since the last time the sandstorm cleared." Fuse shrugged. "Or maybe they've always been here—it's not like we know much about the Great Barren."

"So what now?" Hex was ashamed to hear the slightly hysterical note in her voice. In the past few days she'd faced goblins, ogres, and fairies. But Shades were the creatures of nightmares, the reason people were scared of the dark. Nobody knew what they looked like because they emanated darkness like a thick fog that cloaked them in total, utter black.

Her parents never told her or her brother about Shades, but Hex knew all the stories. They were whispered on the playgrounds at school or in the middle of the night at sleepovers. Shades were made of shadow and evil. Shades were older than the world itself. Shades couldn't hear, but reacted to light and touch. And when some unfortunate person accidentally ran into one or panicked and cast a Light spell? That's when the Shade would come to life and wrap the person in its cold grip, suck up their life, and turn them into a Shade themselves.

Hex shuddered. "Do you think the Thunder Knight knows how to get through safely?" She was really thinking of Cam. Fuse seemed to be thinking the same thing because an unfamiliar expression flitted across her face. It took Hex a moment to recognize what it was. Fear.

"Mr. Sandy Paws must be able to smell the Shades," Fuse said. She waved a hand airily, but Hex wasn't fooled by her dismissive attitude. "And the Thunder Knight cares too much about himself to just barge his way through. I'm sure he's taking it slow and careful. The real question is how are *we* gonna get through?"

"Right. They don't move unless we wake them . . . so we just need to avoid them. In pitch black. Without accidentally touching them." Hex gulped.

"Right. Easy," Fuse said flatly.

They both fell into thoughtful silence before Hex spoke again. "What about a brainstorm?"

"Yeah . . . maybe. Cam would know if we've got something to sense stuff in the dark." Fuse sighed. "I probably should've paid more attention to classes other than chemistry back in Clank City."

"Maybe there's something in *The Curious Book of Clank*?" Hex asked.

They flipped through the book, huddling over it together.

"Wait, turn back a page," Fuse said while they looked through the chapter on electronics. "Proximity sensors—I kinda remember that from class. They let you sense how far away something is without touching it."

"That's perfect," Hex said. They looked through the large trunk in the back of the car until they found a small box labeled *Proximity Sensors* in Cam's messy scrawl. It contained an assortment of sensors in different shapes and sizes.

Fuse picked out a few black cylindrical ones. "Ultrasonic sensors," she said. "We did a project with these in class."

It took a few tries to build it—Fuse didn't have Cam's knack for electronics—but between Hex, Fuse, and the book, they finally managed to build a circuit with the proximity sensor. Fuse pointed the sensor into thin air, then at Hex. As soon as it faced Hex, it started to beep. That part had been Hex's idea. They'd attached an electronic buzzer like Cam had used in the goblin prison so it would beep when the proximity sensor saw something. Since Shades couldn't hear, it was safer than using an LED to indicate when something was nearby.

"All right," Fuse said, taping their device to the front of the car. They made a second one that Hex could use to scan the area around the car while Fuse drove. "We're gonna have to take this slow because the sensor only has a range of a few feet."

Hex swallowed hard and nodded. If Fuse was even half as scared as Hex was, she hid it well. They drove at a crawl and the moonlight faded darker and darker until they were in pitch black.

"Fuse?" Hex's voice sounded thin and small. Even though she knew Fuse must be sitting right beside her, Hex felt like she was the only person left in the world.

"I'm here," Fuse said, her voice close and reassuring. Hex wanted to grab Fuse's arm, but she didn't want Fuse to know how scared she was. Instead she squeezed her necklace so tight her knuckles hurt.

Beeeeeeeeep.

Hex's heart practically leapt out of her throat. Fuse stopped the car.

"Hex?" Fuse prompted. Fuse's calm voice brought Hex back to herself, and she swept the second proximity sensor to either side of the car.

"We're clear on our sides," Hex said.

Fuse turned slowly to the left. Hex kept the proximity sensor pointed in the direction of the Shade. The sensor made a steady beeping noise. How big was the Shade? Was there more than one? Hex wasn't sure she wanted to know.

The beeping stopped so suddenly, Hex jumped a little in her seat.

"All right, I'm gonna turn again so we're still going in the right direction," Fuse said. She turned and Hex expected at any second to feel a cold grip wrap around her throat. But the car kept going, and both sensors remained silent.

"There we go, we just got past our first Shade! That wasn't so bad." Fuse sounded almost cheerful and for a second, Hex was glad for the pitch black so Fuse couldn't see the sweat soaking Hex's dress. "I need to check the compass to make sure we're still going the right way."

"But the light—" Hex croaked.

"Don't worry, we've got a blanket. I'll turn the light on underneath." There was some shuffling as Fuse felt around and then a swish of fabric. Hex held her breath, terrified the light would shine through the blanket. But a moment later there was another rustle and Fuse started driving again. "We're good."

"Yay," Hex said hollowly.

It was a few minutes before they heard another beep. Once again, they made their way around the Shade slowly, Hex checking its location with the handheld sensor, Fuse's calm voice guiding her. They kept going. Hex lost track of how many Shades they encountered. Every time she thought they were safe, they'd hear another *beeeeeeeep* from the proximity sensor and her heart would stop all over again.

"Hey, I think I can see the moon again," Fuse said. Hex looked up. It was so faint that if Fuse hadn't also seen it, Hex would have thought she might be imagining the dim orb in the sky. The fear squeezing her ribs seemed to loosen a little. "We're almost out—"

Beeeeeeeep.

"Seriously?" Fuse demanded, hitting the brakes. She sounded more frustrated than scared.

Hex didn't reply but waved her sensor around like she had before, making sure the path around them was clear.

Beeeeeeeep.

"Um, there's one on our left also," Hex said. She turned the sensor to the right side of the car.

Beeeeeeeep.

"And our right." Hex's voice came out as a whisper.

"That's fine, we'll back out slow and careful," Fuse said. "They don't move unless we accidentally touch one, but want to check behind us just in case?"

Hex swept the sensor to the back of the car.

Beeeeeeeeep.

Beside her, Hex felt Fuse tense. When she finally spoke, her voice sounded strained. "Well, that's . . . not supposed to happen. Maybe us humans don't know as much about Shades as we think we do."

"Now what?" Hex asked.

"I don't know, you've been the one who comes up with the plans so far," Fuse said.

"How fast can the car go?" Hex asked.

"Oh nooo," Fuse said. "I do *not* like where this is going."

"Well?"

Fuse sighed in resignation. "The fastest we've ever gotten it has been like fifty miles an hour. But we're on sand. That'll slow us down. And we have no idea how big or fast the Shades are."

"If they surrounded us, it means they've been moving anyway." Hex shuddered at the idea of the Shades slowly creeping up on them.

"If we turn on the headlights and the Thunder Knight is anywhere nearby, he'll see us," Fuse pointed out.

"Got any other ideas? We're almost out of Shade territory," Hex said. "Chances are the Thunder Knight's already well ahead. And we'll switch the lights back off as soon as we're out of here."

"All right, it's your funeral," Fuse said.

"Uh. You realize you're stuck in the same car with me?" Hex said.

"Good point. Well, you know what they say—you can't spell funeral without 'fun'!"

"Fuse, *nobody* says that."

"They should. Ready?"

"No," Hex said.

"Great!" Fuse slammed on the headlights. Hex had only the briefest glimpse of a large black mass and shadowy tendrils shooting toward them before the car exploded forward. Hex hung on for dear life as Fuse swung the car right and left, swerving around Shades that whipped past them too quickly for Hex to get a proper look at them. Black feelers reached for the sides of the car, but Fuse stayed focused on the growing light ahead, brow furrowed and a determined grin on her face. Large amorphous shadows slithered toward them at startling speed. But the car was faster. They were leaving the Shades behind, and the moon was getting brighter and brighter. They were so close.

Something icy cold wrapped around Hex's neck. She tried to scream but nothing came out. Something had hooked her heart from the inside and was dragging it out of her, leaving her fingers numb and her blood sluggish and chilly. The dissipating darkness closed in on her again, hungry and heavy. It was taking her.

"Fuse—" she tried to say, but it fell from her lips like a soft exhale.

Then they burst into starlight and out of the fog of darkness that marked the edge of Shade territory. The Shade's grip ripped away as the car pulled ahead, leaving the inky sea of black behind. Silver moonlight flooded Hex's senses. She barely even registered Fuse turning off the headlights and bringing the car to stop. Fuse let her head fall back on the seat, eyes closed, breathing hard.

"You realize we might be the first people ever to see Shades and get out alive?"

Hex tried to reply but her mouth wasn't working.

"Hex? Hex, you all right?" Fuse winked an eye open lazily, then both eyes slammed open. "Did one of them get you?"

"Without a shadow of a doubt," Hex said weakly.

"What?"

"That we're the first to see Shades and get out. Without a *shadow* of a doubt." Hex let out a shaky chuckle. "Shadow. Get it?"

Fuse stared at Hex, looking increasingly concerned. Then she started to laugh, and then the two of them were laughing so hard tears rolled down their cheeks. "Hex, your jokes are so bad they hurt."

"Well," Hex said, collapsing back onto her seat bonelessly, "you know what they say—you can't spell punishment without 'pun'!"

A SHOCKING SHOWDOWN

Sometime in the very early morning, Hex caught her first glimpse of the Wishing Wyrm's volcano looming ahead, a craggy mountain of black in a sea of moonlit silver sand. They drew closer and closer until Fuse finally slowed the car down, keeping enough distance so the Thunder Knight wouldn't hear their motor. They continued driving until the first hints of sunrise, when Fuse stopped the car long enough to dig out a metal and glass device that looked like two joined tubes. She handed it to Hex before starting the car again.

"Look through those," Fuse said. "They're binoculars—they work like a Magnify spell."

Hex looked through the binoculars at the volcano. "I think they're broken. Everything looks even smaller!"

"Try turning them around," Fuse said, smirking. "And spin that knob until it stops looking blurry."

Hex did, and every nook and cranny in the volcano came into sharp focus. She saw a small dark patch at the base—an opening.

Not too far from the volcano, she could see Mr. Sandy Paws continuing his journey, his loping gait reduced to an exhausted jog.

"I can see them. They're close." Hex bit her lip. "I think the Thunder Knight knocked Cam unconscious . . ."

Fuse's face fell. Then her scorched eyebrows lowered in determination, chasing away the worry in her eyes. She brought the car to a halt. "They'll hear us coming in the car. Let's run from here."

Hex's heart drummed a nervous beat as they raced toward the volcano. To her left, Fuse carried the potato cannon. Hex had a second cannon which was a modified design. She also had her backpack—if this plan worked, she would be leaving Fuse and Cam, so she'd need all her stuff with her. If the plan didn't work . . . well, they'd both packed some food and water and some clank from the metal chest, so they could survive the desert if something happened. When Hex offered to return *The Curious Book of Clank*, Fuse waved her off and told her to keep it. "Not like I need it," she said dismissively, but Hex didn't miss the significance of the gesture.

They stopped behind a large outcropping of black stone just as the Thunder Knight dismounted and dragged Cam's limp form behind him.

Fuse peeked around the edge of the outcropping. "The lion's guarding Cam, and the Thunder Knight's headed toward the hole in the volcano. We gotta move fast if we want a shot at that wish."

"We?" Hex asked without thinking.

"Me and Cam," Fuse corrected, grimacing. "Once the Thunder Knight goes down, you're on your own."

Hex nodded. "Let's do this." She whipped out a small mirror and angled it so the morning sun bounced off and cast a spot of light on the sand, bright against the shadow thrown by the stony outcropping.

"I hope you're right about this."

"Mr. Sandy Paws is a cat," Hex said with far more confidence than she felt. "I don't know much about lions, but I know about cats. Anyway, I have a good *feline* about this."

"Sparks, do you ever stop?!"

"I'd be *lion* if I said I did!"

Fuse slapped her forehead with her palm.

The idea had come to Hex while she'd been thinking about home. That led her to think about her parents, Spanner, her room, her wall full of drawings . . . and Queen Fuzzybutt III.

Hex aimed the spot of light to where the enormous shadow of Mr. Sandy Paws loomed over Cam's prone form. She wiggled the mirror so the patch of light bounced around like some kind of weird glowing insect. Mr. Sandy Paws looked up sharply. His head twitched right and left as he tracked the movement of the light, his body tense. Then he pounced.

"Gotcha," Hex whispered to herself. Mr. Sandy Paws held

his paws on the sand, looking far too pleased with himself. The Thunder Knight turned around to look at the lion, and Hex quickly ducked back around the rock.

"What are you doing, you stupid animal?" the Thunder Knight bellowed.

Mr. Sandy Paws didn't even acknowledge the knight. Instead, he lifted his paws carefully to inspect his prey. The light, of course, had disappeared the moment Hex had hidden. The Thunder Knight shook his head in frustration and continued trudging toward the entrance carved into the volcano.

Mr. Sandy Paws looked utterly bewildered. He flicked his head one way, then the other—how had his prey escaped? He bounded across the sand, searching. Hex aimed her mirror again. Mr. Sandy Paws spotted the light and pounced on it once again with a low, determined growl.

"Almost there," Hex said. "The Thunder Knight's not looking."

Fuse nodded, and this time, Hex bounced the light all the way back to their hiding spot. Mr. Sandy Paws was so absorbed in his chase, he didn't even notice the two girls until Fuse gently touched his snout. The lion flinched and started to open his mouth but Fuse pressed a finger to her lips.

"Shh—we're Ari's friends. You can go home, I know she's worried about you. "

The lion glanced uncertainly back at the Thunder Knight.

"We won't let him hurt you or Ari," Hex added.

Fuse cracked her knuckles. "We're gonna show him what happens when you mess with Clanksmiths."

Mr. Sandy Paws licked their cheeks, then turned around and galloped back through the desert with a triumphant roar.

The Thunder Knight spun around sharply at the noise. His eyes widened as they landed on Hex and Fuse, then a syrupy sweet smile spread across his face. "Your tenacity is . . . endearing, but this has gone on long enough." His eyes flicked to Cam, but Fuse stepped out from behind the rock, loading a potato into the cannon threateningly.

"Mr. Sandy Paws isn't here to help you anymore," Fuse growled.

"I hope you like mashed potato," Hex said.

"Please, the potatoes again? We don't need to fight." He spread out his hands in a conciliatory manner. "If you behave, I will make sure your contribution to humankind by aiding my ascension to immortality is mentioned in a footnote in the history books."

"Yeah, yeah, we all heard your little speech. Anyway, I want to be remembered for doing something that *helps* humanity," Fuse sneered.

The Thunder Knight's smile withered. "I will not hold back merely because you are children."

"And we won't hold back merely because you're an unimaginative buffoon," Fuse said, and the Thunder Knight's face twitched.

Fuse and the Thunder Knight moved at the same time. Fuse shot a potato out of the cannon just as the Thunder Knight thrust his hands out and shouted, "*Shield!*" An enormous shimmering blue shield bloomed in front of him, and the potato bounced off harmlessly.

It took the Thunder Knight a moment to comprehend the significance of what had just happened. He stared at his outstretched hands in wonder. Hex and Fuse exchanged quick glances. Of course, they'd hoped the Thunder Knight wouldn't have his magic so they could just pummel him with potatoes now that Mr. Sandy Paws wasn't there to protect him. But they hadn't counted on it and had planned for the worst. The Thunder Knight let the shield drop and a viper grin spread across his face.

"It seems the legends about the curse breaking and magic becoming even more powerful in the presence of the Wyrm are true." He inhaled deeply, like he was breathing in the magic and letting it flow into his body. Then he lifted both arms and uttered a spell, low and ominous. It was one Hex had never heard before, one she was almost certain wasn't anywhere in *Spellman's Dictionary*.

"*Storm.*"

They heard a soft, silken sound, as if the very desert itself was taking a breath. And then a dark cloud rose like smoke out of the Thunder Knight's raised arms, spreading over the desert sky. Hex shivered as the temperature dropped and the wind howled, carrying with it stinging grains of sand.

"Fuse, you ready for this?" Hex hissed. Fuse nodded, shoving another potato into the cannon. Then the storm—dry as the desert but dark and furious as the ocean—rushed at them.

Hex and Fuse ran in opposite directions. The wind screamed, and Hex could hardly see through sand whipping through the air, but she heard the *fwoop* of the potato launching from the cannon, followed by the Thunder Knight's bark of laughter. Hex pulled one of several bulging water balloons from her pocket—the same balloons Cam had given her when they'd first met. She shoved it down the barrel of her own cannon, but didn't shoot it just yet. She had to wait for the right moment.

"I have to admit, you are both quite fun," the Thunder Knight said, swimming in and out of view through the windswept sand. "But I'm bored of this game."

The Thunder Knight extended both arms, his palms facing Fuse. The storm had a life of its own now, freeing his hands to perform other spells. His smug smile was barely visible through the churning sand, but Hex knew what was coming next. After all, what was a storm without thunder and lightning?

The first spark of blue-white electricity crackled above his palm. Hex aimed her cannon. She hoped this worked. The salt water that filled the balloon, Fuse had explained, was easy for electricity to travel through.

The Thunder Knight opened his mouth. *"Lightni—"*

Hex shot the cannon, and the balloon careened out of it.

It exploded against the Thunder Knight's hands, salt water splashing against his palms and gushing over the blue sparks of lightning. In that brief moment when the lightning and his soaking wet hands were connected by water, the electricity zipped through the closed circuit and into the Thunder Knight's body. He spasmed, once, twice, then crumpled to the ground. He was still breathing, but he was definitely unconscious.

Hex collapsed to her knees in relief. They had a clear path to the volcano and to the wish. Now they just needed to wake up Cam and . . .

Oh.

Hex looked up at Fuse. She still stood, gripping the potato cannon hard. Her posture was tense, and her eyes were stony with a hard, angry determination.

Hex started to stand up, but Fuse moved so quickly Hex didn't even have a chance to react. Fuse pinned Hex to the ground and jabbed something that felt like a bee sting into Hex's arm. Fuse's scrawny frame hid a sinewy strength, and Hex couldn't move. Fuse's eyes still held that driven look, but the anger faded, and her expression softened.

"I'm sorry, Hex," she said, pulling a needle from Hex's arm. "I told you—I'll do anything for Cam."

Hex opened her mouth to speak. Then her world went blurry around the edges and she sank into darkness.

AN A-MAZE-ING REVELATION

Hex blinked open her eyes. Confusion gave way to a rush of fury, but it faded quickly. As angry as she wanted to be at Fuse's betrayal, it wasn't like when Fuse had sold her out to the ogress. This time, Hex understood why she had done it.

Fuse had left her an extra bottle of water, and Hex took it as a sign that, despite their rivalry, the Clanksmiths weren't going to leave her to die in the middle of the desert.

She stood up. The Thunder Knight's unconscious form still lay where they'd left him, but Cam was gone. He and Fuse must already be inside the volcano, on their way to the Wishing Wyrm. Hex let out a long sigh. It was over.

She should be crushed, shouldn't she? She'd come all this way for her wish. Now she would never be normal. She'd never be able to do magic, go to school like Spanner, or have a job. She felt drained, resigned, and disappointed—but there was also a sense of relief. She didn't have to deal with the guilt of taking Cam's wish.

Somehow, she had managed to hang on to her backpack throughout everything. She opened it to assess the damage. A layer of sand coated the top, but otherwise, everything was still in its place. She took out some food and water and left it by the Thunder Knight, because as much as she loathed him, she still wanted him to get home safe. Then she pulled out *The Curious Book of Clank*. Something about its weight was comforting. It felt even more significant now that she knew her last chance to do magic was gone. She started to put it back in her bag, on top of her sketchbook, then stopped. *The note.*

Hex tore her sketchbook free of the backpack and flipped to the page where Cam had left his note. She unfolded it and read it. Then her eyes widened, and she stood up suddenly, trembling.

Don't worry about your wish. I'll make sure you get it so you can live the life you want with your brother. —Cam

Despite the desert heat, Hex felt cold. Without entirely understanding why, she stuffed the sketchbook back into her backpack and took off for the volcano at a sprint.

Cam would give up his wish for her. Shouldn't that make her happy? Her thoughts reeled in confusion—what *did* she want?

Cam never asked anything for himself, except for one single wish. She didn't know what it was, but she knew she didn't want him to give it up for her. She had to get there first to stop him. Or to beat him? Hex shook her head, trying to clear her thoughts.

What if she accepted his act of kindness? It would do so much not only for her, but for her family. Her mother, stressed from working late hours trying to save money for her. Her father, old before his time, who loved and supported Hex but worried about her. Herself, and how she'd never be able to live a normal life.

And Spanner, even though he believed she could do everything and more. Spanner, who she would do anything to protect. Spanner, who she would cross deserts and fight monsters to see again. Who she couldn't imagine her life without.

And suddenly Hex knew what Cam's wish was.

She ran through the opening of the volcano and into a cavern that was dimly lit by the harsh desert sun outside. Two openings were carved into the rock before her, one leading into a narrow corridor, the other shut by a stone door.

Hex pushed on the door but it didn't budge, so she went into the open corridor. As she stepped forward, a stone door slid shut behind her. The Clanksmiths must have gone through the other door. She hoped they both led to the same place.

She made it about five steps in before her face smacked into something hard. She stumbled back, rubbing her nose where she'd hit it.

Cautiously, Hex raised a hand in the direction she'd been walking and touched a solid barrier. Her eyes told her there was nothing but an empty corridor. But her hand told another story.

It was an illusion. An illusion of a corridor where there was actually a wall. She prodded the air with her fingers, walking in a slow circle. To her left, another wall. But to the right she felt nothing—except that her eyes told her there was solid stone.

Hex closed her eyes and took a step to the right. She opened her eyes. The wall was now on her left—she'd walked directly through it. She breathed in awe. This was powerful, ancient magic. No human could create an illusion so complex. This was the magic of the Wishing Wyrm.

Hex walked slowly, her hands out in front of her. She kept her eyes closed since they were lying to her anyway. At one point, she nearly tripped when her foot hit a rock. She opened her eyes and saw a clear path. But when she reached down, her hand bumped against a large stone with a smooth domed surface. She went around it and continued.

A few minutes later, her foot hit something again. She swept her hands around, fumbling to see what she'd hit, and was horrified to feel the same domed rock as before.

She'd already been here.

Hex opened her eyes. Nothing looked familiar, and yet she was certain it was the same stone. The illusion overwhelmed her and she sank to the ground, trying to ignore the stinging sensation of tears. She was scared of being stuck here, but she was more scared by the idea that Cam would give away his wish before she could get there. Why didn't she want that?

Her thoughts were muddled and loud and confused. She took a long, shaky breath to calm herself.

"Once upon a time, there was a girl who was different from all the other kids." The whispered words came unbidden, her voice shaky and small. "They could banish the darkness with a single incantation, or start a fire with a snap of their fingers. This girl couldn't do any of those things. This girl was No Magic Girl."

Hex stood up. She could think her way through this situation. She *had* to.

"One day, No Magic Girl decided she didn't want to be No Magic Girl anymore. She went on a quest to find a dragon who could grant a single wish, a wish that could heal her inability to do magic. But not long after she began her quest, she met an unusual boy. Like No Magic Girl, he couldn't do magic either. But unlike her, he *could* banish the darkness. With his help, No Magic Girl learned how she too could make light without a single incantation."

Growing up, Hex would have given anything to do something as basic as make a light. She remembered too many nights when she had to get up—to use the bathroom or get a glass of water—and bumbled her way around in the darkness, unable to cast a Light spell, terrified of what unknown demons hid in the dark.

Hex's voice grew stronger as she continued her story. "The boy had a best friend. No Magic Girl learned from her too, and how she could start a fire with the mere flick of a lighter. But there was one problem: the boy and his best friend also wanted the wish from the dragon. No Magic Girl didn't know what to do. Did she go and find the dragon anyway?"

While her mouth moved automatically, her brain continued its frantic churning. The problem was that Hex was picking a direction at random every time she ran into a wall. She could be going in circles, not even realizing there was an exit nearby. And a light wouldn't help her—not with the illusory walls and paths.

On those nights when she had ventured out of her room in the dark, she learned to follow the corridor by keeping a hand against the wall. This really wasn't so different. If she picked one wall and followed it, it would eventually lead somewhere. And if she kept following the wall every time she reached a corner, she would never double back on herself, assuming the path didn't loop.

She set off again, extending her right hand in front of her and running the other hand against the wall on her left. Occasionally she opened her eyes, only to find herself walking through stone or hanging over a chasm when her feet told her she was on solid ground.

"And then she started to wonder to herself, did she even need magic? No Magic Girl used her wits and creativity to solve problems. But she'd only learned to do that because she didn't have magic to rely on. If the dragon changed her, would she even be herself anymore?"

Her hand hit a wall in front of her. There was another wall to her left, which meant she was at a corner. She paused a moment, thinking, then rotated ninety degrees, always keeping her hand along the wall to her left.

With her eyes closed and her steps slow and careful, she couldn't judge how long she'd been walking through the maze. Ten minutes? Twenty? An hour?

Eventually, her foot struck something and she opened her eyes. Before her lay another chasm, too wide to jump across. The remains of a footbridge hung in a rotted tangle of rope and wood from rusted metal posts on either end of the chasm. The ledge on the other side was almost a yard lower, and just beyond it a dark opening was carved into the rock.

Hex reached out a tentative foot, expecting her toes to hit stone. They didn't. She swallowed a gasp and scrabbled backward. Then, more cautiously, she knelt over the edge of the void and tried to touch it. Her fingers swept through thin air. This chasm was real— but with the illusions, there was no way to know if it was only half a foot deep, or hundreds of feet. Hex dug through her pocket, found a screw, and dropped it into the abyss. It was a long time before she heard the faint *ping* of metal on stone.

This time, Hex didn't need to brainstorm or sketch her idea. She touched her NO MAJIK GURL necklace, the memento of all the stories she'd shared with her brother. She knew what to do. She'd already written this story.

Hex took out her rope and tied a loop on one end, then threw the loop across the chasm. It took her four tries before she managed to get it around the metal post on the other side. She gave the rope a strong tug and it held, firm and steady. Then, she took a pulley from the box of clank Cam had given her and tied a short piece of rope to it.

Her first rope-slide had failed when the scarf she'd used as a handle tore. But she'd learned from her failure and understood now how to fix it. The scarf hadn't been able to support Spanner's weight. But this handle was made from the same type of rope she'd used to pull the beam out of Grundzilla's door. If it was strong enough to haul a block of wood many times her weight, it would certainly hold her.

She threaded the pulley onto the longer rope, then pulled the rope taut and tied the other end to the remains of the bridge post beside her. Cam had said she should learn from her failures to make her next design better. As she sat on the edge of the void and gripped her makeshift handle, she hoped she'd gotten this design right. She leaned onto the handle. The rope that was stretched across the chasm sagged but held her weight.

Spanner was going to love hearing about this.

Hex took a deep breath, closed her eyes, and pushed off the edge.

THIS CHAPTER WON'T DRAGON TOO LONG

It was over before Hex even had time to scream. She smacked into the other end of the chasm and pulled herself up over the ledge. Her legs trembled, and it took her a minute before she felt steady enough to stumble away from the edge. Her breathing still ragged, she stepped through the opening in the rock and entered an immense cavern, its ceiling dripping with stalactites. Cam and Fuse were nowhere to be seen.

For a moment, Hex thought the cavern might still be part of the illusion. Then its shadowy depths resolved themselves into a massive black body. Vast wings the size of sails were folded tight against a sleekly scaled torso; a horned head the size of the Clanksmiths' car softly exhaled hot smoke. The Wishing Wyrm.

Slowly but unmistakably, the dragon's eyelids pulled back. It blinked its huge eyes drowsily, then fixed its piercing golden gaze on Hex. Hex wondered for one terrified instant if the dragon, instead of granting her wish, would simply eat her. She took an involuntary step back, but the dragon didn't move to attack.

"You're a clever one," said the Wishing Wyrm in a voice still thick with sleep. "Your friends had a half hour head start on you, but they didn't think of your algorithm until about ten minutes ago. That means you get the wish, little one."

"I, uh . . ." Hex froze, stunned. A million questions raged through her head at once, and somehow the least important one of them floated to her tongue. "My algo . . . algo-rhythm?"

"Ah yes, you're still very new to clank, aren't you?" the dragon replied. Its voice was low and warm, and it drew out each word in a slow, lazy way. "You used a wall-following algorithm. The ancient Clanksmiths used to do the same to get through my labyrinth. But they haven't visited me in a long time."

"Are my friends all right?"

"Oh, yes. They'll be here soon. But the wish is yours, little one."

"It's mine . . . ?" Hex said, her mind still not processing its words. "I could be . . . normal?"

"Normal . . . an interesting choice of word," the dragon said. "If that is what you wish, yes."

Hex's legs wobbled, and she sank to the ground.

The dragon made a strange huffing noise, and Hex realized it was chuckling. "It's not so easy, is it, little one?"

Hex barely registered its words. Her thoughts whirled so furiously she thought she might cry, or laugh, or maybe her head would just explode. She'd run away from home so she could wish to be normal. But she'd run into the volcano because of Cam's note.

A clatter of footsteps echoed through the cavern. Cam and Fuse appeared from a tunnel on the other end of the dragon's lair. They skidded to a stop when they saw Hex. Even at a distance, Hex could see Fuse's mouth fall open and her eyes go wide. The stricken look she gave Hex was a mixture of anger and hurt, like her entire world had just been swept out from under her. But Cam beamed at Hex.

From the moment he'd met her, Cam had looked past what Hex couldn't do and had seen what she could. He'd changed the people closest to him by sharing his love of clank. Clank had brought Hex's stories to life and opened her eyes to a universe of possibilities, which let her shape the world around her, unbound by the limitations of whatever incantations existed in *Spellman's Dictionary*.

Hex had left home so she could use magic. But she never really needed magic. She had creativity and resourcefulness, persistence and curiosity. Spanner and Cam had always seen that. It was Hex who hadn't.

The dragon looked down at her, its eyes wise and knowing.

Hex stood up, one hand closed tightly around the necklace Spanner had given her. "Wishing Wyrm," she said, her voice ringing loud and clear throughout the stone cavern. "I wish to see Cam reunited with his brother."

The dragon's eyes glittered, and Hex thought it was smiling at her. Then her vision filled with white.

* * *

The white light faded from Hex's eyes, and she took a moment to reorient herself. Had it worked? Had the dragon granted Cam's wish? Where *was* she?

Cam and Fuse materialized on either side of her, looking just as confused as she felt. They were in a city, although Hex hadn't the foggiest idea where. Despite the fact they'd materialized out of thin air into a busy market street, no one seemed to have noticed anything strange. People pushed past them as usual, ignoring them as they would any other passersby. Vendors sold pixie traps, dragon fruits, wool from color-changing sheep, and other wares out of stalls with brightly colored awnings. All around them people haggled and laughed and talked. It was so . . . ordinary.

Cam rubbed his eyes. "Where are . . ." He trailed off, staring at something. Hex followed his gaze. With the crowds of people, it took her a moment to realize what he was staring at.

Farther down the street, examining some thaumium charms in a stall, stood a man and a young boy with the same brown skin and black hair. The boy glanced in their direction. Hex's breath caught. It was Cam's face, but younger.

Fuse punched her shoulder. "You gave up your wish." She had an uncharacteristically soft smile on her face. "Thank you."

Hex's lips curved up even as she tried to ignore the lump of emotion in her throat. "Cam needs his brother, just like I need mine."

Cam was oblivious to them. Despite the shifting crowds that

kept cutting through their line of sight, the two boys held each other's gazes. Cam stood rooted to the spot, and Hex saw he was trembling. The boy looked at his father, who was busy arguing with the shopkeeper. Then he took one hesitant step toward Cam, then another. A familiar lopsided smile spread across his face as he broke into a run.

NO MAGIC GIRL RETURNS

"You gonna be okay?" Fuse asked. "I mean, on account of not being able to do magic? I know your home isn't like Clank City. Regular folk don't seem to think you can do anything if you can't do magic."

She and Hex walked down a bustling road to the carriage station. It was loud and busy enough that as long as they kept their voices low, they didn't need to worry about anyone overhearing their discussion about clank.

The car had been left behind in the Great Barren, so Hex's only way home was the long carriage ride back to Blinkenburgh, then on foot from there to Abrashire. She wondered if the car was still sitting in the middle of the desert, or if the Thunder Knight had figured out how to drive it.

"I'll just have to show everyone they're wrong," Hex said. She touched her necklace. "Anyway, I'll manage. Clank can help me fix my problems, but it couldn't have helped Cam find his brother. He needed that wish more than I did."

"You did a good thing, Hex," Fuse said.

Hex's cheeks warmed up. "I guess the Wishing Wyrm thought so too. The legends say it'll only cast the wish on a single person, but it transported all three of us so we could be together."

Cam was waiting for them on a bench outside the carriage station. He leapt to his feet when he saw them and wrapped them both in an enormous hug. He was dressed differently—his goggles were gone, and he wore a staid button-up vest in dark blue instead of his usual lime green. Hex didn't like it one bit, but she knew he was trying to impress his father.

"How's it working out with your dad?" Fuse asked.

Cam pressed his lips together, troubled. "Um, well, he still doesn't seem too happy to see me."

"And what about your brother—Barrel?" Hex asked.

Cam's entire demeanor changed. He opened up like a flower, and the smile that spread across his face could have lit a thousand ogre caves. "He's amazing. I told him everything, about Clank City, how I met Fuse and then you, how we got to the Wishing Wyrm . . . and how you gave up your wish for me." He lowered his face, but not before Hex caught his shy expression. "Thank you," he said softly. "I don't know how I can ever repay you."

"Cam, you've already repaid me." Hex took his hand and squeezed it. "You made me a Clanksmith."

Cam looked up and beamed at her.

"You sure you don't want to come to Clank City with me?" Fuse asked. "Or go with Cam once he's sorted things out with his dad and brother?"

Hex shook her head. "I can't. Not yet."

Fuse shrugged as though she'd been expecting that, and Cam nodded solemnly.

The carriage pulled up in front of them, and Hex's chest tightened. "I guess this is goodbye then?"

Fuse snorted. "You don't think you can wiggle your way out of homework that easily, do you?"

Hex laughed, bewildered. "What do you mean?"

"Soon as I get to Clank City, I'm loading up a car with books and clank for you and driving right back to Abrashire," Fuse said. "Cam and I already decided. That way you can keep learning at home."

"And I'll come visit," Cam promised. "And Barrel too."

"Th-thank you," Hex said, stunned and overwhelmed. She started to enter the carriage but stopped. Instead she threw her arms around them, hiding her face so they wouldn't see the tears stinging the corner of her eyes. "Thank you," she said again, before stepping into the carriage.

Fuse grinned. "See you 'round, No Magic Girl."

EPILOGUE

"Hex, will you tell me a story?"

Hex rolled over as Spanner climbed into her bed. He had grown taller in the months since Hex's return, but his sweet, eager smile was the same as it had always been. "Sure, Spanner. Which one do you want to hear?"

"The one where you tricked the ogress!"

"Again?"

"Yes! But I want to see the picture!" Spanner reached toward the lantern Hex had built and pushed the button. The room filled with light, exposing the partially built robot on the floor, the rubber band flying machine on the dresser, the cardboard catapult, and all the wires and batteries and gears and bolts scattered across their shared desk.

The room was a disaster, but her parents didn't seem to mind. In fact, they'd even cleaned out one of the closets so Hex could store her creations. They still worried about her, but they didn't worry like they had before. They knew she had a future, even if it might eventually be far from home. They understood—Hex was a Clanksmith.

Hex wrapped an arm around Spanner as he opened her sketchbook to one of the newer drawings. Someday, she knew, she would go to Clank City. Maybe not tomorrow, or the next year or the next, but someday. And when he finished school, maybe Spanner would come with her. She didn't know what the future held, but it didn't scare her anymore.

"Once upon a time, there was a girl who was different from all the other kids. They would panic if they were kidnapped by goblins, or freeze in fear if an ogre tried to eat them. This girl wouldn't do any of those things. She saw solutions where normal people only saw problems and she used nothing but a handful of clank and her imagination to create things that had never been made before. This girl was No Magic Girl."

THIS SKETCHBOOK BELONGS TO:

THE **FUN**NELATOR

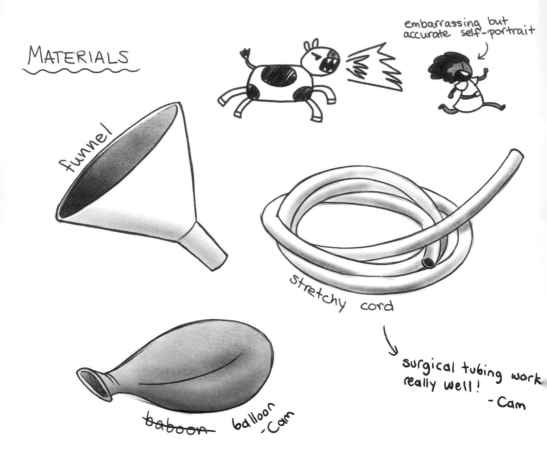

MATERIALS

funnel

embarrassing but accurate self-portrait

stretchy cord

surgical tubing work really well!
- Cam

~~baboon~~ balloon
-Cam

① Put two holes on each side of the funnel. It's easiest if you have a drill.

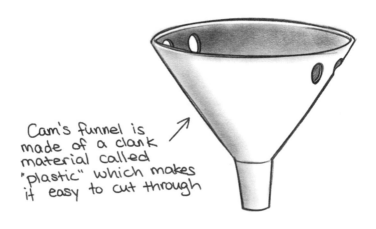

Cam's funnel is made of a clank material called "plastic" which makes it easy to cut through

② Put the stretchy cord through the holes in the funnel

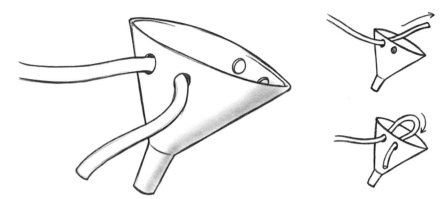

③ Tie both sides of the stretchy cord into loops. It's <u>knot</u> hard!

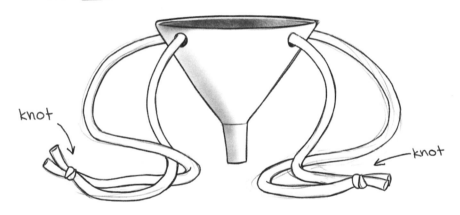

knot

knot

④ Fill the ~~baboon~~ balloon with water.

⑤ LAUNCH IT!!!

HEX ALEN

"LIGHT THAUM"

(actually an LED but don't tell Grundzilla!)

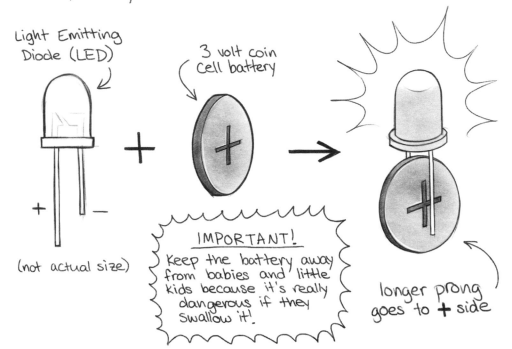

Light Emitting Diode (LED)

3 volt coin cell battery

+ −

(not actual size)

IMPORTANT!
Keep the battery away from babies and little kids because it's really dangerous if they swallow it!

longer prong goes to + side

How it works:

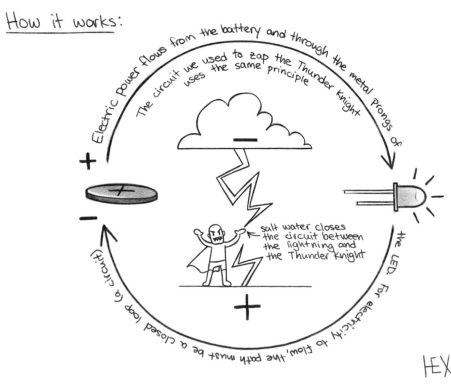

Electric power flows from the battery and through the metal prongs of

The circuit we used to zap the Thunder Knight uses the same principle

salt water closes the circuit between the lightning and the Thunder Knight

the LED. For electricity to flow, the path must be a closed loop (a circuit)

HEX ALEN

OGRE READING LIGHT

(or a night light for humans)

↑ because Light Thaums are totally <u>ogre</u>-rated

MATERIALS

frosted or clear jar

a cup, bottle, or anything else that lets light shine through also works!

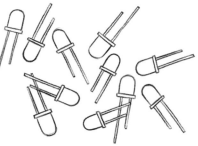

LEDs (in your favorite color!)

sticky ribbon

tape -cam

3 volt coin cell batteries

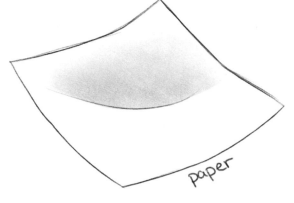

paper

① Bend the LEDs at an angle

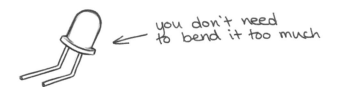

← you don't need to bend it too much

② Use the sticky ribbon to attach the batteries to the LEDs.
More LEDs = brighter lamp

make sure the longer wire is on the + side of the battery

(if the LED turns off, make sure the sticky ribbon is still holding the wires down)

This type of LED is brightest at the top, which is why I bent them so the top points out.

③ Use the sticky ribbon to attach the LEDs to the inside of the jar. I put some on the lid and some on the bottom.

It's got lights now, but it doesn't really look like a lamp yet. That's because we still need something to spread the light more evenly.

or frosted
plastic —cam

④ Frosted glass works well to spread the light, but if you're stuck in an ogress cave and only have a clear jar, you can wrap a thin sheet of paper (or colorful tissue paper) to the outside instead.

You can use sticky ribbon or glue to attach it.

⑤ Put the lid on and read a good book!

You don't have to do it exactly the same way I did. You can experiment with your own design

decorate the paper!

put LEDs on the inside walls instead of the top and bottom!

⑥ You can save batteries and make an even BRIGHTER lamp if you use an LED strip!

—Cam

LED strip (all the LEDs are attached)

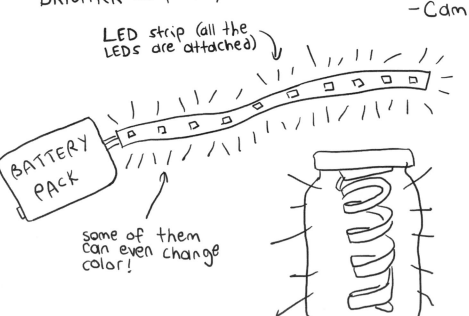

BATTERY PACK

some of them can even change color!

HEX ALEN

How To Pick Up Really Heavy Stuff

(aka "How to break out of an ogre cave")

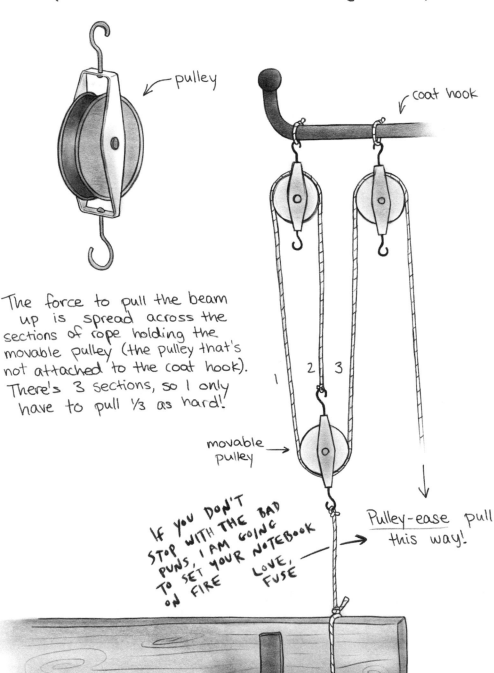

pulley

coat hook

The force to pull the beam up is spread across the sections of rope holding the movable pulley (the pulley that's not attached to the coat hook). There's 3 sections, so I only have to pull ⅓ as hard!

1 2 3

movable pulley →

If you DON'T STOP WITH THE BAD PUNS, I AM GOING TO SET YOUR NOTEBOOK ON FIRE LOVE, FUSE

Pulley-ease pull this way!

Because you rotated the beam out, you also had the mechanical advantage from torque. But that's a whole other lesson...

— Cam

You woodn't believe how heavy this was!

THAT'S IT.

If you don't have pulleys, you can do this with hooks or carabiners but it will be harder to pull because of friction

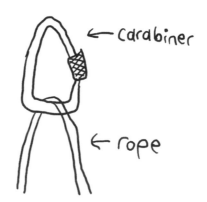

← carabiner

← rope

HEX ALEN

MOTORIZED CART
written by Cam, drawn by Hex

There's a bajillion ways to make a motorized cart. Here's how Fuse and I did it with just the stuff in my pockets

MATERIALS:

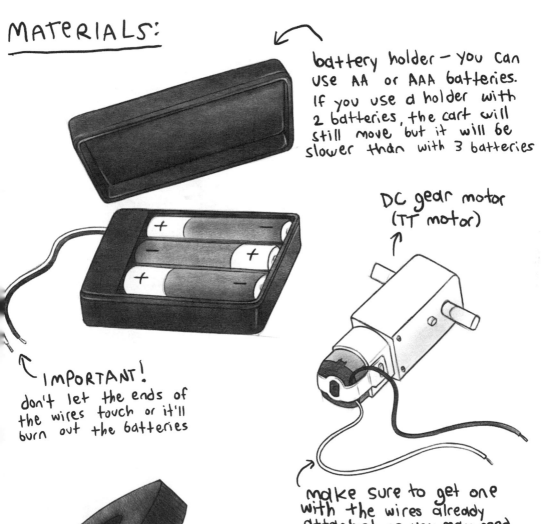

battery holder - you can use AA or AAA batteries. If you use a holder with 2 batteries, the cart will still move, but it will be slower than with 3 batteries

DC gear motor (TT motor)

IMPORTANT! don't let the ends of the wires touch or it'll burn out the batteries

make sure to get one with the wires already attached, or you may need to find a more experienced Clanksmith to help you solder the wires on

tape
electrical tape or duct tape work well

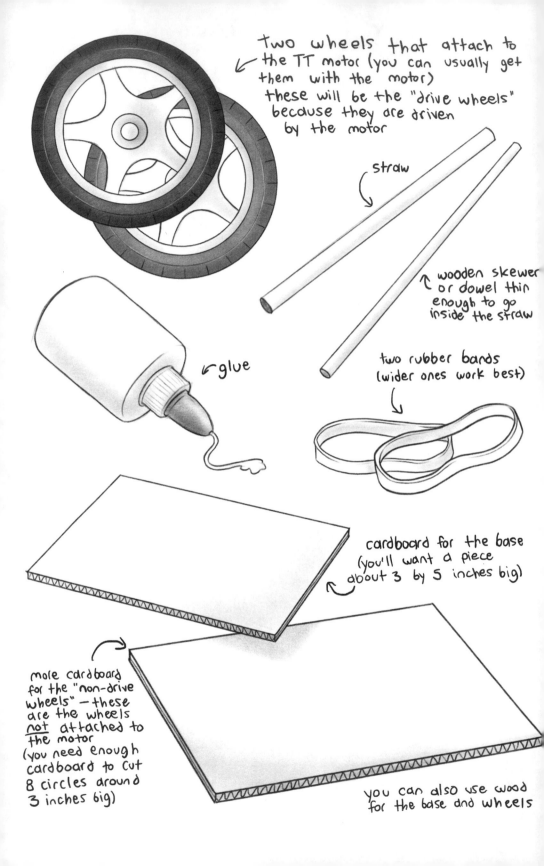

two wheels that attach to
the TT motor (you can usually get
them with the motor)
these will be the "drive wheels"
because they are driven
by the motor

straw

wooden skewer
or dowel thin
enough to go
inside the straw

glue

two rubber bands
(wider ones work best)

cardboard for the base
(you'll want a piece
about 3 by 5 inches big)

more cardboard
for the "non-drive
wheels" — these
are the wheels
not attached to
the motor
(you need enough
cardboard to cut
8 circles around
3 inches big)

you can also use wood
for the base and wheels

1. Put the motor on the base and mark around it where the dotted lines in the picture are.

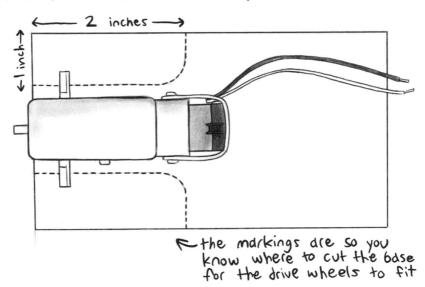

← 2 inches →

← 1 inch →

← the markings are so you know where to cut the base for the drive wheels to fit

2. Cut out the parts you marked.

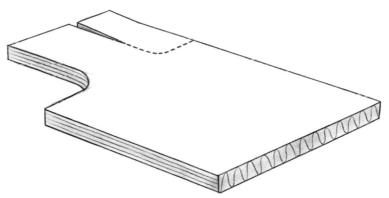

3. Tape the motor to the base.

make sure the side of the motor with the wires faces inward ↙

4. Attach the drive wheels to the motor.

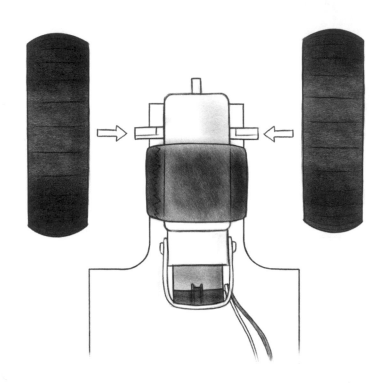

5. Cut the straw so it's a little wider than the base, then tape it to the base.

6. Cut out 4 circles from the cardboard, about the same size as the drive wheels →

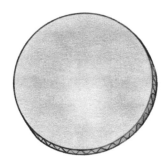

7. Glue the cardboard circles together to make a non-drive wheel. Then put a rubber band around the edge so the wheel is grippy.

They're <u>wheel</u>-y easy to make!

-Hex

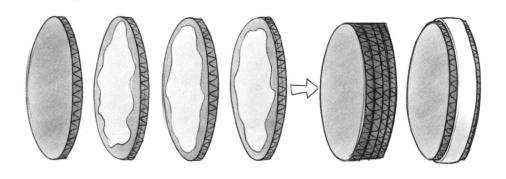

8. Repeat steps 6 and 7 to make another non-drive wheel.

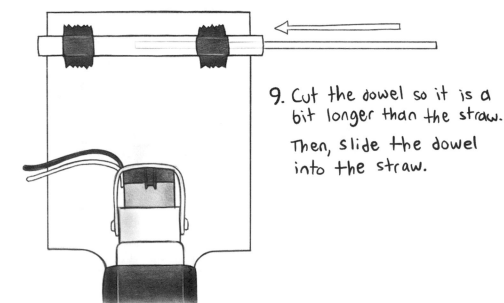

9. Cut the dowel so it is a bit longer than the straw.

Then, slide the dowel into the straw.

10. Attach the non-drive wheels by pushing them onto the dowel so it makes a hole in the middle, then putting glue to hold it in place.

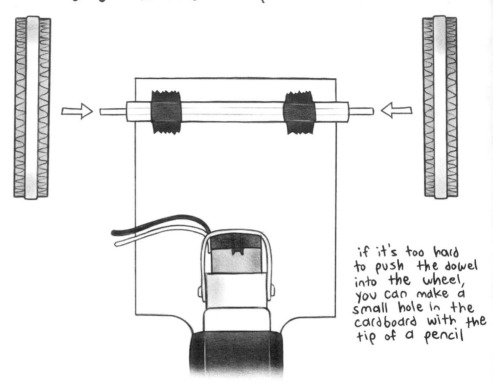

if it's too hard to push the dowel into the wheel, you can make a small hole in the cardboard with the tip of a pencil

11. Flip the cart over and tape the battery pack on.

make sure it's turned off

12. Attach the motor wires and battery pack wires together. Match black to black wire and red to red wire. If you want the wheels to spin the opposite way, then do red to black wire instead.

If your wires already have built-in connectors, attach them like this:

If your wires don't have connectors, you can attach them like this:

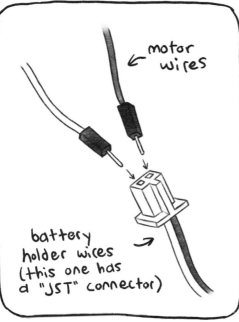

← motor wires

battery holder wires (this one has a "JST" connector) →

twist the ends of the wires together then tape them

When I'm in Clank City, I use solder to attach wires. Solder is more secure, but this also works in a pinch!

If some wires have a connector and others don't, you may need to get creative, or find a more experienced clanksmith to help you.

13. Turn on the cart and watch it go!

Cam L.
HEX ALIEN

GOBLIN ANNOYER

Buzzers come in different types and sizes. The one Cam used was a piezo buzzer with an internal driver. I have no idea what that means...

piezo = the type of buzzer
internal driver = all the circuits
    to make it work are built in
                        — Cam

The buzzer works like the LED – you can attac it directly to the batter

the red wire goes to the **+** side of the battery

the longer prong goes t the **+** side o the battery

I used the sa battery fro the LED

BEEEEEEEEP

HEX ALE

JAIL-BREAK ELECTROMAGNET

MATERIALS:

copper wire

we used a D-cell battery to ~~steal~~ borrow the key, but a smaller battery works too, it just won't be as strong

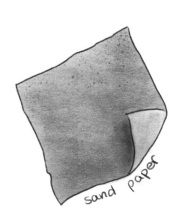

D-cell battery

wood from old goblin shelves

tape →

I still think "sticky ribbon" is a better name

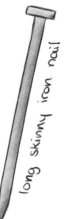

long skinny iron nail

sand paper

① Wind the copper wire around the nail. It helps to use a piece of tape to hold the wire in place for the first few winds.

wrap it neatly so the wire winds don't overlap too much

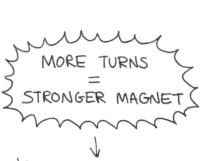

MORE TURNS
=
STRONGER MAGNET

the one Cam and I made had around 100 turns of wire

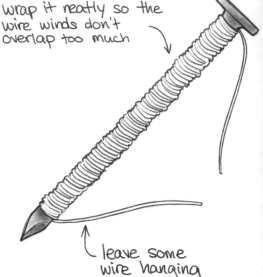

leave some wire hanging

② Sand the ends of the wire to take off the coatin (the coating stops it from conducting electricity).

the wire ends will look shinier and light when the coating is o

sandpaper

Tape the nail to a battery.

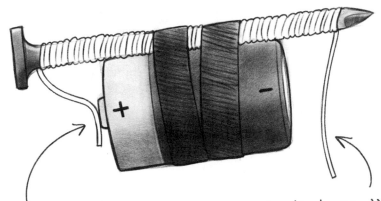

tape one end
of the wire to
the battery

don't tape the
other end until
you're ready to
use it. Cam says
the electromagnet
drains the battery
pretty fast!

4) Make a stick using the old goblin shelves
and some tape.

tape the electromagnet
to the end

Recipe for Fuse a la carte:
Ingredients:
   1 pun-hating Clanksmith
   2 buckets of suspicious-
      looking red sauce
   1 vat of Bert's favorite
      brown marinade
   3 spoons of the spice mix
      on page 33 of Bone Appétit,
      issue 413

m positive the
ey will stick to
his!

I'M POSITIVE YOUR
JOKES ARE AWFUL
         — FUSE

No need to be so
negative!   —Cam

⑤ Tape the other end of the wire to the battery to turn it on, and take the key!

IMPORTANT

Don't keep the wire attached to the battery for long because it gets **HOT**!

How it works!

When electricity goes through a wire, it causes a weak magnetic pull. By winding it around a bunch, you concentrate that pull to make it stronger.

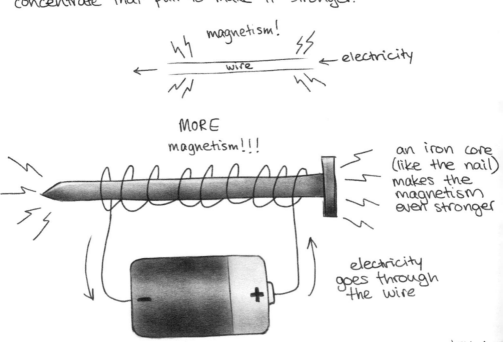

magnetism!

wire

← electricity

MORE
magnetism!!!

an iron core
(like the nail)
makes the
magnetism
even stronger

electricity
goes through
the wire

HEX ALE

FUSE'S ESCAPE ROUTE USING UV-SENSITIVE LIQUID

DRAWN BY HEX, WRITTEN BY FUSE

TONIC WATER

UV LED.
THERE'S ALSO UV FLASH LIGHTS, SOMETIMES CALLED "BLACK LIGHTS"

TONIC WATER HAS A CHEMICAL CALLED QUININE THAT COMES FROM TREE BARK. UNDER UV LIGHT, QUININE GLOWS BLUE.

HOW IT WORKS

ULTRAVIOLET (UV) IS A KIND OF LIGHT THAT WE CAN'T SEE ("WE" AS IN HUMANS. I DON'T KNOW IF GOBLINS CAN SEE IT). WHEN YOU SHINE UV ON TONIC WATER, THE QUININE IN IT GIVES OFF LIGHT THAT WE <u>CAN</u> SEE

UV light (invisible)

blue light (visible!)

I can see it now!

FUSE + HEX ALEN

SHADE DETECTOR

This project uses a lot of advanced electronics that I don't entirely understand. Fuse and I managed to figure it out using *The Curious Book of Clank* and what Fuse remembered from her electronics class in Clank City, but don't be afraid to ask a more experienced Clanksmith for help with this one.

MATERIALS:

breadboard

This is just a board that you use to build circuits. The wires plug into the holes in the board.

An ultrasonic sensor is a type of proximity sensor. It's used to figure out how close something is (like if there's a Shade in front of it). You'll need the help of an experienced Clanksmith to solder on the "header" (pins). You can also use press fit or solderless headers instead.

ultrasonic sensor (Maxbotix LV-EZ)

NPN Transistor

specifically, you want a → BC547B transistor

Transistors and resistors are pretty high level electrical clank. You don't need to understand exactly how they work, but basically they help the circuit decide if something is too close to the ultrasonic sensor and make the buzzer beep if it is.

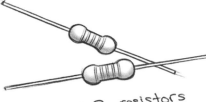

5.6 kΩ resistors (you'll need 2)

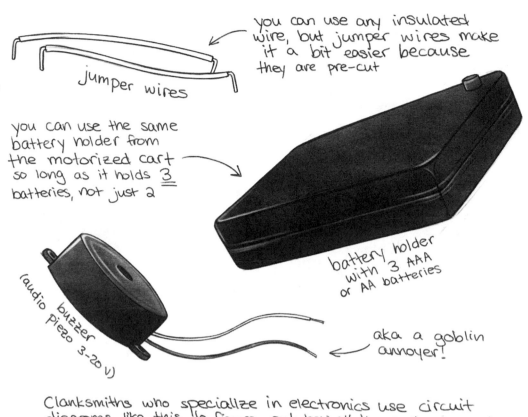

you can use any insulated wire, but jumper wires make it a bit easier because they are pre-cut

jumper wires

you can use the same battery holder from the motorized cart so long as it holds 3 batteries, not just 2

battery holder with 3 AAA or AA batteries

(audio buzzer piezo 3-20 v)

audio buzzer

aka a goblin annoyer!

Clanksmiths who specialize in electronics use circuit diagrams like this to figure out how all the parts connect

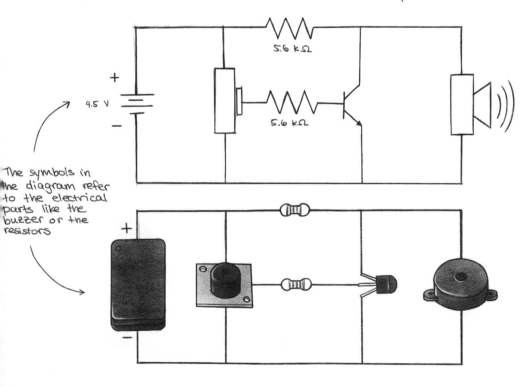

5.6 kΩ

4.5 V

5.6 kΩ

The symbols in the diagram refer to the electrical parts like the buzzer or the resistors

+

−

To make the Shade Detector, you'll want to copy the layout of the breadboard <u>exactly</u>, otherwise it won't work. (Unless you're working with an experienced Clanksmith. They'll know how to change it so it still works.)

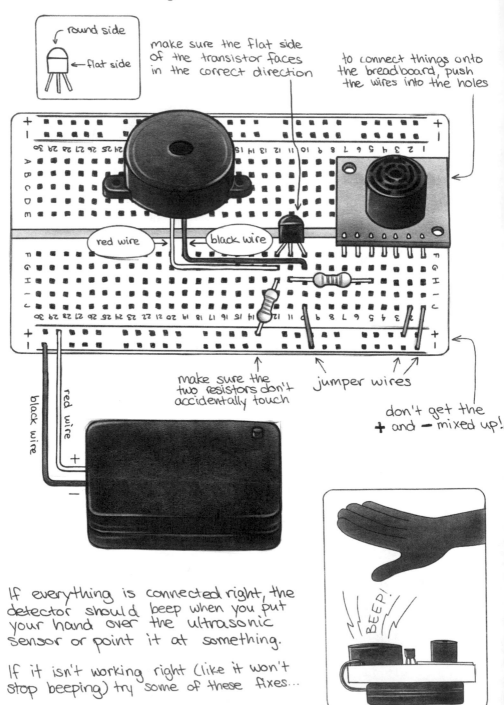

round side
flat side

make sure the flat side of the transistor faces in the correct direction

to connect things onto the breadboard, push the wires into the holes

red wire
black wire

make sure the two resistors don't accidentally touch

jumper wires

don't get the + and − mixed up!

black wire
red wire
+
−

If everything is connected right, the detector should beep when you put your hand over the ultrasonic sensor or point it at something.

If it isn't working right (like it won't stop beeping) try some of these fixes...

BEEP!

If it won't stop beeping:
- The sensor may be detecting the ceiling. Try putting it on the floor, or pointing it away from anything.
- Try using new batteries

If it won't start beeping:
- Make sure all the connections are right
- Check that the batteries aren't dead

The sensor has a long range so it can detect shades before they get too close. You can figure out the range by pointing it at someone or something, then moving backwards until it stops beeping. That's when it's out of range.

How IT WORKS by Cam

The ultrasonic sensor uses soundwaves to detect if something is in front of it. It lets out a sound that is too high-pitched for us to hear and if there's something in front of the sensor, the soundwaves bounce back off and into the sensor. The sensor knows how close something is based on how long it takes for the soundwave to bounce back.

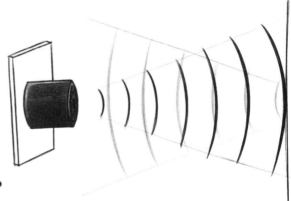

The transistor acts like a switch. When something gets too close, it sends an electrical signal to the buzzer to make it beep.

HEX ALEN

POTATO CANNON

HOW IT WORKS:

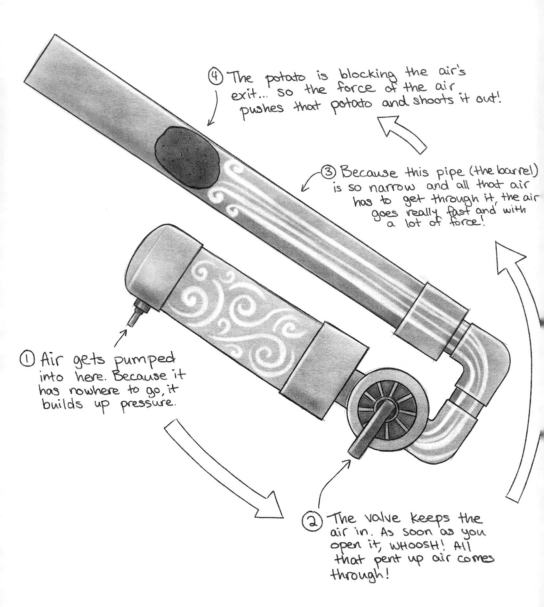

④ The potato is blocking the air's exit... so the force of the air pushes that potato and shoots it out!

③ Because this pipe (the barrel) is so narrow and all that air has to get through it, the air goes really fast and with a lot of force!

① Air gets pumped into here. Because it has nowhere to go, it builds up pressure.

② The valve keeps the air in. As soon as you open it, WHOOSH! All that pent up air comes through!

The water balloon cannon works in a similar way, though I put some water down the barrel to cushion the balloon so it doesn't burst when it shoots out

Potato cannons and water balloon cannons can be dangerous because of the pressurized air. Just to be safe, I'm not including the instructions for how to make them (in case someone who's not a Clanksmith reads this).

Instead, here's a marshmallow shooter Spanner and I built that also uses air power!

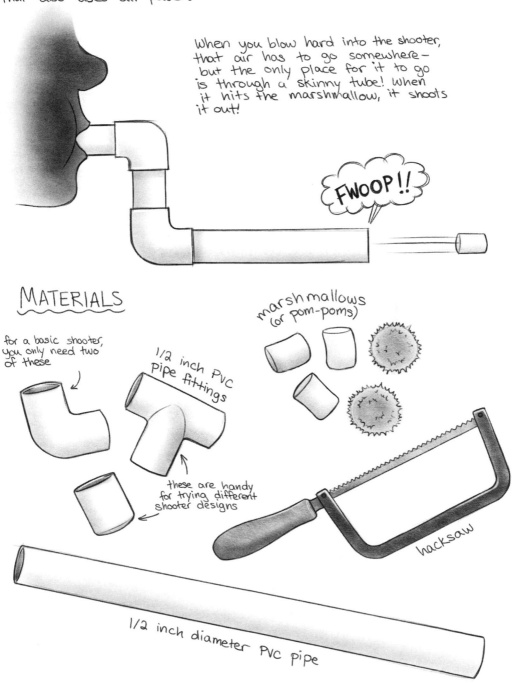

When you blow hard into the shooter, that air has to go somewhere— but the only place for it to go is through a skinny tube! when it hits the marshmallow, it shoots it out!

FWOOP!!

MATERIALS

for a basic shooter, you only need two of these

1/2 inch PVC pipe fittings

these are handy for trying different shooter designs

marshmallows (or pom-poms)

hacksaw

1/2 inch diameter PVC pipe

① Use the hacksaw to cut the PVC pipe. For a basic marshmallow shooter, cut 2 short pieces and one long piece.

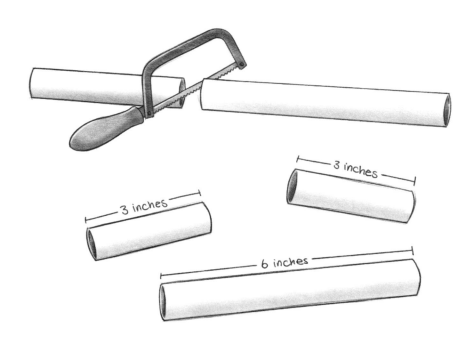

├── 3 inches ──┤

├── 3 inches ──┤

├────── 6 inches ──────┤

② Assemble the shooter! The pipe should squeeze into the fittings tight enough that you don't need glue.

Don't forget to wash off any small bits of plastic from cutting the pipe or they'll get into your mouth (ew!)

③ Load a marshmallow (or a pom-pom) and BLOW! Spanner and I found that a short, sharp puff of air works best.

Spanner and I tried loads of other shapes also, to make it easier to aim or more comfortable to hold. You can try inventing new designs too!

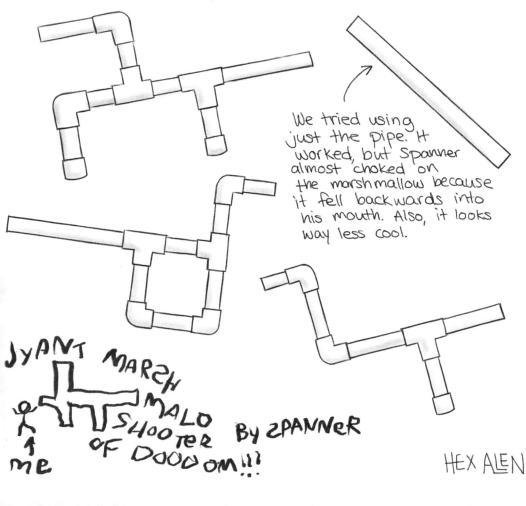

We tried using just the pipe. It worked, but Spanner almost choked on the marshmallow because it fell backwards into his mouth. Also, it looks way less cool.

JYANT MARSH MALO SHOOTER OF DOOOOM!!!

BY ZPANNER

me

HEX ALEN

HOW TO ESCAPE A LABYRINTH

(or find the bathroom in the dark)

The Wishing Wyrm called this a "wall following ~~algo rhythm~~".
Cam says it's for computer programs (whatever those are).
The trick is to always turn so my left hand is against the wall
that way I don't backtrack by accident.

Left hand: wall
Right hand: nothing

→ Keep going forward!

Left hand: nothing
Right hand: wall

→ Turn right!

This situation really only happens at the beginning, before I've found a wall to follow

Left hand: nothing
Right hand: nothing

→ I'm at an outside corner! Turn left!

Left hand: wall
Right hand: wall

→ I'm at an inside corner! Turn right!

What if the labyrinth had loops?

Lucky for me it didn't, or I'd have been going in circles forever! That's because with the algorithm, I always turn so my left hand is on the wall.

I wonder if the Wishing Wyrm made it that way on purpose?

How robots use the wall following algorithm:

The robot has proximity sensors (like Fuse and I made to avoid the shades) to tell it when a wall is nearby.

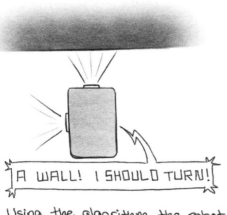

A WALL! I SHOULD TURN!

Using the algorithm, the robot decides which way to go based on what the sensors "see".

The sensors "see" the wall the same way I use my hands to feel it.

HEX ALEN

HOW TO MAKE SMOKEBOMBS
by FUSE

LIGHT IT HERE

VISCO FUSE

SUGAR + POTASSIUM NITRATE

CHECK OUT THOSE EYEBROWS

INSTRUCTIONS

~~1. MIX POTASSIUM NITRATE AND SUGAR IN~~

SORRY HEX, YOUR EYEBROWS ARE TOO NICE FOR YOU TO ACCIDENTALLY BURN OFF SO I CHANGED MY MIND ABOUT GIVING YOU INSTRUCTIONS. I'LL SHOW YOU HOW TO MAKE SMOKEBOMBS WHEN YOU COME TO CLANK CITY.

ACKNOWLEDGEMENTS

This book came into existence only because of all the amazing people who supported me and were generous with their time and expertise.

Thank you first and foremost to Nate, who heard enough about Hex while we were dating to melt his ears off, but married me anyway. Thanks for feeding me all those nights as I stayed up late to write and for helping me come up with silly chapter titles.

Thank you to the Florentine monkeys—Isaac, Ethan, Michelle, and Evelyn—for being so supportive and for critiquing the early drafts of the book. Even if you did lose all the puns, Ethan. Thank you to my mom, Barbara, who never got to read the finished book, but read the very first draft of the very first chapter and immediately emailed back: "STOP SLEEPING AT NIGHT AND USE THOSE EXTRA HOURS TOWARD WORKING ON THIS INCREDIBLE BOOK." She would probably be forcing it on every person she knew right now if she were still alive. And of course, thank you to my amazing uncles, aunts, and cousins for being my biggest fans.

Thank you to the many incredible friends who helped me out with this book. You taught me about the ins and outs of publishing, beta-read the many iterations of the manuscript, lent me your STEM expertise, inspired me with ideas for engineering and science projects, and even test-built the projects in Hex's notebook. I am so grateful to all of you: Graycie, Itaru, Dra, Zach, Marissa, Hannah, David, Anna, Tim, Susan, Murthy, Caitlin, Emily, Soumya, Nelson, Alex, Adina, Robin, Lauren, Sharon, Andrew, Maya, Amanda, Catherine, Yaks, Sarah, Maddie, Ariel, Rachelle, Danbee, Jessica, Stephen, Ami, Michael, Jenn, Tasha, Fowler, Linda, the members of Dublin's TOG hackerspace, and the STEPS Engineers Week staff and participants. It's been a yearslong journey with many people involved, so if I missed you, then please accept my apologies and an IOU in future acknowledgments.

Thank you to all my teachers for inspiring my love of reading, writing, science, math, and engineering.

Thank you to my incredible agent, Jemiscoe Chambers-Black, for believing in my work, having my back, and being so patient with all of my questions about this often discombobulating industry.

And the biggest thank you of all to the Innovation Press and Asia Citro, and the amazing team you assembled: Jolie Stekly, Jessica Petersen, Allison Conner, and Cindy Reeh, who shaped the book into something far, far better than what it started as and taught me to be a better writer along the way. Tim Martyn and Nicole LaRue, who created the whimsical and wonderful design, layout, and lettering. And especially Ebony Glenn, who brought Hex, Cam, and Fuse to life in her beautiful and expressive illustrations. Thank you for infusing them with such color and personality that I can't help but smile every time I see them.

ABOUT THE AUTHOR

JASMINE FLORENTINE likes to make stuff. This has encompassed everything from making ticklish robots out of paper, designing game fields for the FIRST Robotics Competition, inventing a sensor for a brain-scanning race car helmet, drawing comic books (such as her upcoming graphic novels, *The Adventures of Maker Girl* and *Professor Smarts*), and of course, writing books.

She studied mechanical engineering at MIT and is passionate about showing everyone how amazing science, technology, engineering, and math (STEM) are. *Hex Allen and the Clanksmiths* is her first book.

Visit her online and check out more STEM tutorials and resources at www.jasmineflorentine.com.